31 Fantastic Adventures in Science

WOMEN SCIENTISTS of INDIA

Nandita Jayaraj and Aashima Freidog

Illustrations by Upasana Agarwal

PUFFIN BOOKS

An imprint of Penguin Random House

PUFFIN BOOKS

USA | Canada | UK | Ireland | Australia
New Zealand | India | South Africa | China | Singapore

Puffin Books is part of the Penguin Random House group of companies
whose addresses can be found at global.penguinrandomhouse.com

Published by Penguin Random House India Pvt. Ltd
4th Floor, Capital Tower 1, MG Road,
Gurugram 122 002, Haryana, India

First published in Puffin Books by Penguin Random House India 2019

10 9 8 7 6 5 4 3

The views and opinions expressed in this book are the authors' own and the
facts are as reported by them, which have been verified to the extent possible,
and the publishers are not in any way liable for the same.

ISBN 9780143445685

Book design and layout by Devangana Dash
Typeset in Gotham Rounded and Index Pro by Manipal Digital Systems, Manipal
Printed at Repro India Limited

www.penguin.co.in

For my young friends Nitin, Raghav, Aditya and Daria, whose hunger for stories and peals of laughter keep me forever motivated to tell a good story
Nandita

For my niece Ira, a fantastic child who always knows exactly what she wants, and all the other kids who will read this book. Take this along on your adventures
Aashima

INTRODUCTION

Say 'science'. In the time it took you to say that, billions of invisible neutrinos from the sun passed right through you. In the south of India, particle physicist Indumathi is preparing to trap some of these neutrinos using a giant underground facility. Meanwhile, in the far west of the country, a palaeobiologist named Devapriya is crouched over the dry lands of Kutch, hunting for fossils that will help her solve some of the biggest evolutionary mysteries. Not too far away, environmental biotechnologist Vanita's small factory is churning out a secret recipe for microbes for a very special purpose. This is only a tiny peek into the wonderful world of scientific adventures contained in this book.

These thirty-one stories emerged from our three-year journey across India, on a mission to discover Indian women scientists. We have met and written about over 100 Indian women in science and now we bring some of these stories to you. We are two friends, and storytellers, who share a passion for science and feminism. In 2015, when we worked together in an office, we often talked about why there weren't any famous Indian women scientists. We knew that they existed, so why wasn't anybody talking about them? We both wanted to write about the science that Indian women do. But we hardly knew any women scientists. So when we left the office we both worked in, we set off on a journey to seek out the women behind the scientific wheels of India.

Do we ever see Indian women scientists on TV, in textbooks or in newspapers? How many of us can name one contemporary Indian scientist, let alone a woman scientist? Unsatisfied with the answers to these questions, we began a tour across India, peeking in and out of the places where scientific studies are ongoing. We visited the laboratories of dozens of research centres across the country. Some had cutting-edge technology at their disposal and some had to make do with dusty benches and scant reagents. It was not always easy, but there was never a shortage of women passionate about their science.

We met each of them and spent the day talking to them, following them around as they went about their work. We asked them many questions: what was their research about, what discoveries had they made, why did they love science and what had inspired them to become scientists? We also asked them about the difficulties they faced in their lives and work. As a group, it is not easy for women to stay in science. Even though the same number of men and women study science in India, only 14 per cent of scientists are women. Most famous scientists belong

to historically privileged groups like higher castes. Moreover, gender is a spectrum and not all of us identify with the gender binary—man or woman. Sadly, women and individuals who do not identify with this gender binary are even less visible in Indian science. There are many issues behind the gender gap, but in this book, we challenge them and celebrate the women who are contributing to scientific research in India.

Women have always contributed to the human story but when it is time for recognition and appreciation, they are simply ignored, edited out or forgotten. Take Rosalind Franklin, for example. A photograph of DNA that she had instructed her student to take was leaked to two other scientists without her knowledge. This photograph was the breakthrough that led to the discovery of the structure of DNA! But when the Nobel Prize for this discovery was announced, it only recognized the efforts of the two other scientists James Watson and Francis Crick—both men. For many years, until she died, Rosalind's contributions remained hidden. There's every reason to believe that there are similar stories of women scientists in India that have been lost or hidden. It's time to change that. This book is not a historical listing of great women or goddesses but an introduction to amazing women who are doing extraordinary research today. Their work is contributing to the progress of human society. It is time to erase the myth that human progress is all thanks to great, old, white men.

The women featured in this book have been chosen with a lot of thought. They come from various parts of the country. They address scientific questions in diverse fields, from astronomy to immunology. While some peer through telescopes to observe eruptions on the sun, others operate high-tech microscopes to watch cells communicate. In this book, you will also be introduced to researchers working in areas that are specifically crucial to the Indian context—how we deal with our agricultural and industrial waste, the challenges of Indian netizens, identifying the scientific value in traditional technologies that could be revived, and preserving our local environment, flora and fauna. The seemingly random number, 31, is meant to convey a sense of continuity—a tribute to the fact that the scientists featured in this book are only 31 of the thousands of inspirational stories out there.

We are lucky to hail from a country like India where education in science, technology, engineering and mathematics is considered very important. This book is a reminder that just as important is the contributions of historically marginalized groups such as women in science. There is a place for each and every one of us in science.

NATASHA
GURUNG
Horticulturist

Growing flavourful mandarins in the mountains is no easy task—especially if viruses keep attacking your trees. Thankfully, Natasha, the fruit scientist, is working hard in her lab to help the farmers in the hilly northeast make a good living.

SAVING THE MANDARINS

In the Himalayan town of Kalimpong, Natasha works at an agricultural research centre, lovingly called 'The Virus Office'. Natasha's hometown is in nearby Sikkim, where the air is cold and crisp, the roads windy and the mountains high. To get from her home in Sikkim to Kalimpong where she now works, she has to go up and down a few mountains. The scenic drive takes about three hours and on the way, she sees many beautiful orchards dotted with bright orange spots, as this is where the famous juicy Darjeeling mandarins grow.

However, all is not well. The number of mandarins that the orchards in the area are able to sell has been decreasing over the years. The spread of a virus that infects mandarin trees has destroyed several orchards. Locals fear that one day, this special variety of oranges with the unique flavour of the north-east will completely disappear. The economy of this area is at risk, since it is dependent on agriculture.

Hill agriculture presents a set of challenges that are not faced by those engaged in agriculture in the plains—Natasha realized this while growing up in Sikkim. These challenges could be dealt with by improving farming techniques. Being a local, she knew she could make a big impact since the people she was working for were her own people, and she knew their troubles well. 'When I went for higher studies, I experienced a whole new world. I realized that in my area, farmers are still following the traditional method of farming. Farming can be very progressive and productive. Whatever I have learned and experienced, I needed to teach my people as I belong to them,' she says.

Many years have passed since then, and that is exactly what she does today. Natasha's work in the Virus Office is aimed at uprooting the viral infection that is threatening the area's hill agriculture. She checks the orchards in the area to identify infected trees. To stop the infection from spreading, the infected trees must be taken down and new virus-free, healthy trees must be planted.

In the field, Natasha also finds some healthy trees with lots of flavourful mandarins. She collects samples with fast-growing cells from infected trees as well as healthy ones and takes them back to her laboratory. In the lab, her team gets to work. First, the virus is identified from the samples collected to make sure no new kinds of diseases have spread since the last survey. Then, Natasha prepares a map of the region, marking the infected orchards and the healthy orchards in the area. She knows that the farmers who own the infected orchards need help.

The fast-growing cells of healthy varieties are multiplied in a technique called tissue culture. From one healthy cell, Natasha triggers the growth of hundreds of plants by growing them in a special jelly in the lab, which is much better than soil. These copies are grown into saplings out on the agricultural centre's farm when they are a little bit bigger. Soon they become ready to be distributed to the farmers who have lost their trees due to the viral infection. As a horticulturist, Natasha also interbreeds different healthy varieties together to get the best trees for Kalimpong.

Natasha knows a lot about diseases that have been spreading among the trees in Kalimpong. She has identified the virus, and learnt how to get rid of it. As a result, some trees can be saved. So, Natasha and her team invite local farmers to the virus office regularly to share with them their new scientific techniques that will keep their orchards infection-free. It is very important to keep the quality of the fruits high. The top-quality varieties are certified as the best by the scientists at the virus office. 'The fruits are part of the legacy of this place,' Natasha says.

Natasha has some interesting scientific ideas to help the farmers. On top of this list is an easy technique to extract citrus oil from mandarin peels that are usually thrown away. To Natasha, this seems like a waste because the peels contain a lot of citrus oil that is useful in the food and perfume industries. Oil from special citrus fruits is bound to be special. If farmers can grow mandarins for oil and not just for the fruit, they will profit more. What a nice idea!

SHARADA
SRINIVASAN
Archaeologist

Archaeology is the study of human history through ruins and objects from a long, long time ago. Sharada is an expert in analysing prehistoric artefacts and uncovering scientific secrets that lurk within local histories.

THE ARTEFACTS IN OUR BACKYARD

The year was 1990 and Sharada Srinivasan had just reached Aranmula, a small town in Kerala. But, unlike most of us, she wasn't drawn to the green fields and backwaters. Instead, she found herself mesmerized by a mysterious artefact that the area was famous for—the *Aranmula Kannadi*.

Aranmula Kannadi is a type of metal mirror which shows reflections better than any glass mirror we use today. Isn't that strange? Its exact composition is a secret known only to a handful of artisans in Aranmula. Metallurgy experts have wondered about the physics and chemistry behind the *Aranmula Kannadi* for a long time. Sharada, an archaeometallurgist, is one of the first and most successful in the quest to find out more about it. Her tests showed that a proportion of tin is mixed with copper to produce an alloy that gives the mirror its reflective powers. Thanks to her investigations, we now know much more about how craftspeople use inexpensive and locally sourced organic materials to produce a high-tech super-reflective mirror. The *Aranmula Kannadi* is just one of the many scientific secrets that lurk within local histories.

Archaeology is the study of human history through ancient material remains. Many of these remains are metallic in nature since metals can stay intact over thousands of years, even if they corrode. In many ways, uncovering the relationship between humans and the metal objects they produced reflects the level of technology that existed at that point in history. It is to study this that the field of archaeometallurgy was born. Sharada's journey into this field of science was not planned, but it seems as though it was meant to be.

Sharada spent her childhood growing increasingly passionate about two aspects of her life—dance and science. She began training as a Bharatnatyam dancer early in life. And thanks to her nuclear scientist father, she had many opportunities to visit nuclear reactors and hear about nuclear fission and fusion. By the time she finished school, she knew that physics was her future calling. She joined one of India's best engineering colleges to study engineering physics. The next few years were spent working on equations and lab experiments. As exciting as a life in physics can be, Sharada soon realized that her spirit did not want to be contained within the lab. *I want to be out there in the open, travelling and having adventures*, she thought.

A conversation with an uncle convinced Sharada that there was a way to bring together her interests in the outdoors, physics and art forms. 'Get out there and document traditional knowledge and crafts. Upgrade them!' he told her. This sounded just perfect to Sharada. She began studying art history and visited many museums containing archaeological artefacts. The scientist in her began wondering how she could use her expertise to study and document cultural heritage and archaeology.

Contrary to what we are led to believe, some of the greatest and earliest advances in metallurgy came from regions that are today called 'developing' nations—China, India and countries of the continent of South America. One of the materials Sharada studies is Wootz steel, a high quality hybrid steel. The technology to produce this existed in India long before the West's industrial revolution. It was so sought after in the 1600s, that it was being exported to Europe, China and the Arab world. Damascus, an ancient city in Syria, imported Wootz steel to make their famous shatterproof Damascus swords.

Sharada was determined to revive this lost history so it would no longer lay forgotten. She began investigating these historical accounts. She identified several sites in southern India where Wootz steel was produced, and studied its composition and physical behaviour. She confirmed that this was indeed a highly advanced material whose properties of superplasticity and high-impact hardness made it globally renowned. Sharada's evidence proves that this traditional technology should be studied in modern metallurgy textbooks.

But studying archaeometallurgy is about more than just adding to textbook knowledge. It's not even about feeling proud about India's past greatness. Valuable ancient technologies existed in many other places around the world and it is important to bring them back into our present-day knowledge systems. Otherwise, we may end up wasting a lot of time reinventing the wheel. Studying archaeometallurgy also reminds us about our rich local histories and encourages us to explore the histories that existed beyond those of the Gupta or Chola dynasties that we read about in textbooks.

For more than two decades, Sharada has been tirelessly gathering information about metals used in the past and the traditional crafts connected to them, which continue to be practiced to this day. She also writes books and makes films about her discoveries. Her big dream is to use all of this knowledge and the artefacts she collects to revive India's museum culture. It's a hard task, but archaeometallurgy surely deserves its own museum, right?

KIRAN MAZUMDAR-SHAW

Biotechnologist

Brewing beer is a technique that has been practised by humans for over 8,000 years—it is one of the most ancient forms of biotechnology developed on earth! It is also the technique that introduced Kiran to the world of business and pharmaceuticals.

Brewing Up a Pharma Empire

As the head of India's largest biopharmaceuticals company, Kiran Mazumdar-Shaw is on a mission: to make high quality drugs available to patients across the globe at a low cost. However, healthcare has not always been on Kiran's mind. As a young girl, she spent many hours accompanying her father to the brewery he ran. He was a brewmaster, the person who supervises the beer-making process in a brewery. Kiran loved wandering inside his beer cellars sniffing the wafting aroma of malted barley.

Passionate about science, Kiran first wanted to become a doctor in order to heal the world. She was disappointed when she could not get admission to any medical colleges. She then turned to her father for advice. 'Why don't you become a brewmaster like me?' he suggested. It was an unusual choice because in those days—the 1970s—very few girls chose to venture into the field of brewing. But the more she thought about it, the more confident Kiran grew about taking this path. After all the hours she had spent watching her father on the job, who could be readier for the job than her!

Brewing, in its simplest sense, is the process of making beer and other types of alcohol. But to Kiran, it was so much more than that. It is a technique that has been practised by humans for over 8,000 years—probably the most ancient form of biotechnology developed on earth! The driver of the brewing process is a type of fungi called yeast. Yeast, like many other microorganisms, contains special enzymes that give it the power to break down carbohydrates. This type of microbial breakdown is called fermentation. Beer is produced when yeast breaks down the cereal barley. Similarly, curd/yoghurt and wine are the results of the fermentation of milk and fruit (mainly grape) juice, respectively.

Smitten by the prospect of becoming a brewmaster, Kiran left India to study brewing in Australia. Being the only woman in her class didn't make any difference to her single-minded focus on her goal. She topped her class and decided to return to India and begin hunting for her dream job. However, back in India, Kiran was in for an unpleasant surprise. Nobody was ready to hire her as brewmaster! She realized that this was because brewing was traditionally seen as a 'man's job'. Disappointed, she began searching for opportunities outside India and was offered one by a company in Scotland. Kiran was getting ready to leave the country again, but a chance encounter changed the course of her life.

An Irish businessman approached Kiran to help him start a business in India. His company was called Biocon and he wanted to manufacture and sell an enzyme that is found in papayas. Papayas are commonly grown in India so the businessman had decided that India was the right place for this to happen and that Kiran was the woman for the job. She did not have experience running a business but the subject of enzymes—a crucial component of brewing—was very close to her heart. Tempted to give it a chance, Kiran agreed to the businessman's offer, but on one condition: if she did not succeed as a business woman, he would have to help her get the job she really wanted, as a brewmaster. So, Kiran set aside her Scotland plans and took over Biocon India's operations.

Biocon India began operating in a garage in 1978. It was very difficult for Kiran in the early days because not many people were willing to work for a female boss. Also, money was scarce as banks refused to loan her money. Nevertheless, the small team, consisting of herself and two retired car mechanics, persisted. In 1979, they began manufacturing papain—the enzyme extracted from papaya—and became the first Indian company to manufacture and export enzymes to the United States of America and Europe. As things began working out, Kiran realized she was falling in love with the challenges of running a business. In 1998, she took over complete ownership of the company Biocon, helped by her husband John Shaw.

Kiran was well aware that healthcare in India needed a revolution and believed that biotechnology could be the answer. So she slowly began orienting her company towards healthcare and pharmaceuticals. When her best friend and her husband were both affected by cancer, Kiran realized how prevalent the disease was in India and how inadequate the available treatment options were. To improve the situation, she started a cancer centre dedicated to providing affordable treatment to cancer patients in India.

Under Kiran's leadership, Biocon has grown into a leading global biopharmaceutical company and India's largest biotech company. It is also Asia's largest producer of insulin, a life-saving hormone for people with diabetes. It now has offices all over the world and employs over 7,000 scientists in its 90-acre Biocon Park in Bengaluru. Kiran is living proof that girls can do anything they set their minds on, whether it is brewing beer or running a giant corporation.

PRAJVAL SHASTRI ~

Astrophysicist

Astrophysicists use science and maths to understand how cosmic bodies like stars and galaxies are born, grow, move and die. Prajval uses these skills to understand one of the biggest mysteries of our universe—black holes.

4

SHEDDING LIGHT ON BLACK HOLES

Nights in Mangaluru were memorable for young Prajval. Sometimes, the family would lie down on mats spread out in the open garden, gazing at the vast skies above. On a clear-skied night, they could see planets and the Milky Way. Once, they were even lucky enough to catch sight of a comet! When she was ten years old, Prajval was thrilled to read that humans had finally stepped on the moon. Yuri Gagarin and Valentina Tereshkova—the first man and woman to travel into space—were Prajval's heroes.

One of Prajval's favourite books was a biography of Marie Curie. In that book, she saw a picture of the scientist in a classroom that was full of boys, except for Marie Curie herself. Prajval wondered why that was so. Science is for everyone, so why weren't there more girls becoming scientists? *It just didn't make sense*, she decided.

When Prajval grew up, she chose to study astrophysics, which is the study of objects in the universe. Astrophysicists use science and maths to understand how things in the cosmos are born, and how they grow, move and change. How did our earth, the other planets, stars and galaxies come to be? One of the most enigmatic features of the universe is the black hole. We know very little about it and Prajval is one of the many astrophysicists in the world trying to shed some light on the darkness.

Black holes can form when giant stars begin to die. There are millions of them sprinkled all over our galaxy, the Milky Way. At the heart of the Milky Way lies a giant black hole, weighing as much as several million suns. Such giant black holes are very common in the centres of galaxies and Prajval is keen to understand how they grew to that size.

The great thing about space is that it's out there for anybody living on earth to access and investigate. Prajval accesses it with the help of a special set of telescopes. Most of these are too large to fit in her bag or even inside her lab. Some are situated in observatories around the world, but her favourite ones are located even further—in fact, they are not even on earth! Instead, they float around in space, undisturbed by the earth's atmosphere and light pollution.

But black holes have no light of their own, so how are telescopes able to see them? Actually, you don't always need to see something to know it's there. Take the wind, for example. You can't see it, but you know it's there when you see trees swaying. Similarly, a black hole can be detected by its effect on the surroundings. Because of its very high gravity, anything that comes close to a black hole is accelerated to great speeds and eventually falls in. So high is the speed and the acceleration, that the matter being sucked in is set alight. Detecting this light is how astrophysicists like Prajval spotted black holes—until April 10, 2019, that is. On this day, astronomers announced that, for the first time in history, they had obtained an image of the silhouette of a black hole. The image clearly shows the ring of light that serves as the most direct evidence for black holes that anybody could hope for.

Light waves come in different frequencies. Light waves of visible and radio frequencies can easily pierce through the atmosphere and reach telescopes on the earth. However, light waves of X-ray and gamma frequencies cannot. This is why, to observe black holes, Prajval needs not only radio telescopes but space telescopes as well. With time, giant black holes suck in more material and grow even bigger. In the process, they also shoot out jets of gas into space, sometimes at speeds nearly as fast as the speed of light. Prajval's calculations suggested that X-rays were being spewed out not just by the matter being sucked in, but also by these jets of gas.

To confirm this, she needed to use a space telescope that can see X-rays. The ROSAT, launched in 1990, was the right telescope for the job. Prajval

needed to point the ROSAT towards gas-spewing black holes and test if her calculations were correct. But these space telescopes are not accessible to everyone. They are few in number and generally shared by scientists around the world, so naturally, the demand for them is rather high. First, Prajval had to prepare a proposal describing what she wanted to use the ROSAT for. If the scientists found her ideas convincing, then would they grant her time. She was thrilled when they said yes to her proposal! She now had a few hours with the space telescope to observe her favourite galaxies with giant central black holes.

The technicians used remote controls to make the space telescope point in the direction of the black holes Prajval wanted to observe. And then, Prajval's calculations were proved to be correct. The jets of gas, being spewed out of the supermassive black holes she observed, all contained a lot of X-rays. Since then, Prajval has used several space telescopes and made discoveries that are telling us more and more about black holes. Now that astronomers have managed to generate an image of the 'invisible' black hole, Prajval believes that the door to a whole new world of investigation has been opened.

5

BUSHRA
ATEEQ
Cancer biologist

As one of the few scientists in India to study prostate cancer, Bushra aims to create a radical change in the way the disease is diagnosed and treated.

COLLECTING SIGNATURES OF PROSTATE CANCER

Every so often, Bushra Ateeq receives emails from around the country asking for advice. Most of these emails are from people who believe that her research on cancer can help cure their loved one of some form of this dreaded disease.

Bushra tries her best to help out, but she always lets them know that, as a molecular oncologist, her research, no matter how ground-breaking, has still not made its way to clinics. However, she is determined that one day it will.

As a little girl, Bushra liked—just for fun—to collect biological samples of grasshoppers, wasps, butterflies, seedlings and such. Once, she even caught a small bird and brought it home. Her parents scolded her for trapping the poor bird, but saw this as a sign of natural curiosity in their daughter. To encourage her interest, they gladly bought her scientific objects like a prism and magnets.

Bushra's mother taught history at a local college in their hometown of Bareilly in Uttar Pradesh. Her friend, Kumud Aunty, a biology lecturer at the same college, not only tutored Bushra and helped her understand difficult concepts, but also whipped up yummy kheer to warm her up as she studied for her exams.

As her interest in biology deepened, Bushra learned about genes and their mutations, which are the small changes that develop in genes. She started her scientific journey by studying the damage that occurs in fish DNA on account of the fish being exposed to chemicals used in agricultural fields. The results of her study horrified Bushra. *If these chemicals can cause so much damage at the chromosome level, surely they might also be affecting the human body when we consume food and water from toxic environments?* she pondered.

This was the moment Bushra's scientific interest shifted from simply studying mutations to studying human diseases like cancer. Cancer is a deadly disease in which cells in a particular part of the body keep dividing, forget to die and cause havoc in the body, often leading to death. Cancer is caused by mutations in genes that we can acquire from environmental toxins or stresses. It can even occur naturally in a person if an error in the DNA goes unchecked or if a person is born with the tendency to develop cancer. Usually, a single mutation is unlikely to cause cancer, but multiple mutations over a lifetime could trigger the disease. Fascinated by the world of cancer biology, Bushra decided that this was the field for her.

Changing your area of research after having done a PhD is not an easy feat—'But if you are driven, there is no limit,' Bushra likes to say. She re-trained herself in cancer biology. After two years of training, Bushra was ready to work on cancer research herself. Over the next seven years, she gathered more experience at famous labs in Canada and the United States of America. Finally, the self-proclaimed 'late bloomer' was ready to return to her country as an expert in prostate cancer.

As the lifespan of the average Indian increases, age-related diseases like prostate cancer become more common. Prostate cancer occurs in a walnut-shaped organ called the prostate gland, which is an organ only those born male have. After oral cancer, it is the second most common form of cancer found in Indian males. By 2020, the number of cases of prostate cancer is set to double. However, as it is a disease that mostly affects men as they get older, it does not receive as much attention as breast or oral cancers. In fact, Bushra is one of the very few people in the country conducting research on this type of cancer.

Bushra wants to steer her research in a direction that will improve the lives of cancer patients as quickly as possible. She is looking for certain gene 'signatures' in prostate cancer patients. These will help clinicians to tailor treatment according to the needs of individual patients. Bushra and her students conduct many experiments with mice in their laboratory to identify gene modifications that could reduce or completely stop the growth and spread of the cancer.

She also wants to change how prostate cancer is diagnosed. In India, at the moment, painful tissue removal is the only way to test whether a person has cancer or not. Often, the wrong diagnosis is made. Bushra believes that she can come up with a less painful way of diagnosing prostate cancer, perhaps through blood or urine. Along with prostate cancer, Bushra's group is also investigating breast cancer and colon cancer. Managing and finding a cure for cancer has been at the top of many scientists' lists. Much progress has been made in the field, thanks to the hard work of researchers like Bushra.

A long time ago, Bushra had told her mother she wanted to join the Indian Air Force. As a patriotic youngster, she wanted to serve her people. She had even passed the written test for the Air Force Selection Board, but had failed the physical test. Today, Bushra has found an equally meaningful way of expressing her patriotism—by contributing to science in a way that will enhance the quality of life of Indians everywhere.

LIPI THUKRAL

Computational biologist

Like all biologists, Lipi makes observations to understand the living world a little better. But as a computational biologist, she substitutes living samples and microscopes for powerful supercomputers.

SUPERCOMPUTING THE CELL

Growing up in north India, Lipi loved biology but found that she did not enjoy doing biological experiments in college. Why? Because they involved standing for long periods. It may sound like a small pet peeve, but Lipi's hatred for standing shaped her future, in a way. Instead of giving up on biology entirely, she started looking for alternative ways in which she could contribute to it. Surely, there must be more to biology, right? Her father pointed out that there was a centre near her home where she could learn computer programming after college and Lipi jumped at the chance. Computer programming or 'coding' was becoming really useful to biologists at that time, Lipi was really good at it, and most importantly, it could be done sitting down!

Software, built by computer programmers, make today's world go round. It allows us to send instant messages to faraway friends, pay our electricity bills without leaving home and run 'smart' electronic appliances like TVs and washing machines. Even in the world of scientific research, software is becoming crucial.

Lipi understood that she could use her talent in computer science to make an impact in the world of biology. Keeping this in mind, she trained in some of the best universities in Europe. Back in India, she started her own lab and recruited a team of scientists to work with her on computational biology. Like all biologists, they design their experiments to understand the living world. But unlike traditional biologists, computational biologists do this without living samples.

Hers is not a typical biology lab. There are neither microscopes nor any test tubes or specimen jars on the desks. Instead, there are rows and rows of powerful computers. On one of these computers, you may find Lipi hunched over, working with software to solve several mysteries of the living cell.

Working with living cells is difficult because cells are microscopic. Powerful microscopes are expensive and even those are unable to zoom in beyond a point. Computer models have no such limits. A skilled computational biologist like Lipi can build models of cells that look or behave very much like real cells but on a computer screen. Though computational biologists can work with various kinds of data, Lipi is most interested in how cells clean up.

Cells are busy chemical factories, constantly building new molecules and breaking down old ones. In this process, a lot of waste is created. Eliminating this waste is the job of a cell organ called a lysosome. Waste materials floating around in the cell get swallowed up by bubbles that travel to the lysosome and get destroyed. This is an important process known as autophagy.

Understanding autophagy could be a game changer in cell biology because this is how cells manage stress. It may even have links to cancer. However, there is still so much we don't know about it. After spending hours deconstructing the cell and its working, Lipi began to wonder—how does a cell know when it's time for a clean-up? And when it's time, which molecules have to work together to make it happen? She knew that the best way to answer this question is to zoom into a cell and actually watch autophagy happening. But this is very, very difficult. There is too much happening inside a cell and at sizes and timescales that are too small for us to observe. This is why Lipi built a computer model of autophagy.

Building a computer model takes a lot of skill and computational power. A cell, though considered tiny, is still made up of millions of molecules. Lipi's model had to consider every single molecule or else it would be useless.

To maximize her chances, she used a supercomputer situated in another city. The hard work was worth it. With her computer model of the autophagy system, Lipi could zoom in as much as she wanted to. She finally began to understand how it works. She predicted that a molecule called LC3 is needed for autophagy and discovered the exact parts of it that do this job.

Before she could celebrate, Lipi needed to test her discovery. She was confident that her computer model was good, but in science, all results need to be cross-checked. She approached her cell biologist friends and asked them to do the same experiment but on real cells. After a hopeful wait, Lipi could finally celebrate. Her prediction about LC3 was true! Now she is even more confident about the power of computers to solve big problems in biology. Will humans ever have the cell completely figured out? With cell biologists and computational biologists working as a team, Lipi has no doubt that the day is not too far away.

ARCHANA LAKHANI

Condensed matter physicist

Extremely low temperatures and very high magnetic fields make materials behave in strange ways. As a condensed matter physicist, Archana performs many tests and checks on various combinations of materials to find these strange behaviours that just might bring the next big leap in digital storage.

EXTREME MACHINES, EXTREME PHYSICS

Archana grew up in the ancient temple city of Ujjain. As a school girl, she spent her time solving math problems and thinking about the laws of thermodynamics. At university, she was no ordinary student. She topped her class in all three of her undergraduate years.

After graduating, she wasn't sure which subject to pursue—physics or mathematics. She was good at both. She believed herself to be a thinker and liked the way physics made her think. Solving math problems logically, step by step, was also fun. But she preferred to visualize the laws of nature, so she chose physics.

Archana began her life as a scientist by researching superconductivity—the property of some materials to conduct electricity without any resistance when they are cooled to very low temperatures. What we consider normal room temperature is around 300 kelvins or 26.5 degree Celsius. Archana started working on a machine called the Dilution Refrigerator whose temperature can go down to millikelvins (1 kelvin is 1000 millikelvins.). This bagged her a job in the United Kingdom, developing the coldest refrigerators in the world.

Her work there was exciting but Archana longed to do her own research using the amazing machines she was developing. And she did just that. She came back to India, to Indore, in her home state Madhya Pradesh, and joined the same scientific institute where she had done research for her PhD. Here, she has her own lab where she is surrounded by high-tech scientific technology.

The institute Archana works at specializes in testing out the unusual properties of materials under unusual conditions. It has lots of expensive, complex and high-tech machines that are hard to find anywhere else in the country. These machines can take different measurements from samples of metals, alloys, compounds and newly invented complex materials at very, very low temperatures and in high magnetic fields. Under these extreme conditions, the materials act in very strange ways and physicists like Archana like to observe them being strange.

Archana is the only woman at her institute. And it has been this way for more than ten years now. Some people incorrectly think that girls are not good at conducting physics experiments, but Archana has been proving them wrong every day. Laboratories from around the country send their material samples to Archana's lab. Here, she tests them, and shares the results with students and researchers from various universities, institutes and colleges.

On the door to her lab is a big sign that says: 'DANGER, High Magnetic Field'. Inside the airy room, the walls are decorated with posters explaining Archana's experiments. Tanks full of liquid nitrogen and liquid helium that can take temperatures down to 77 kelvins and 4.2 kelvins respectively, stand in the corner next to the window, along with a heavy-duty instrument housing a big magnet.

Archana's experimental conditions of low temperatures and high magnetic fields reveal interesting properties of the materials she tests. By studying these properties, Archana can find how many electrons are present in a sample, for example, in a small piece of iron. She can also determine how fast the electrons are moving in this piece of iron.

But why do such experiments matter? 'So that we can invent new technology easily,' says Archana. Knowing the hidden properties of materials she tests allows her to find new uses for these materials. Her goal is to invent the next generation of electronic devices such as more powerful digital storage devices for computers, phones and hard disks.

The materials Archana likes to study express a property called GMR—giant magnetoresistance. Her favourites are new materials called topological materials that hold a promise for advancement in the future of computers. These materials are special because their electrical conductivity can be controlled by a magnet. They can be used to imprint digital data on them.

Earlier, people used floppy disks and CDs that held not more than 700 megabytes of data. But now we have hard disks that hold up to 16 terabytes of data. 'Digital storage devices could hold more and more data over time because better materials with better properties are being used to make them,' Archana explains.

But nowadays, physicists like Archana, who work with materials, cannot take digital storage much further unless there is another big discovery. This keeps Archana busy with different combinations of materials in her experiments. She enjoys these very much.

One of the properties Archana is very keen on researching is the one that she started with—superconductivity. Superconductivity at room temperature has never been seen before. When it does happen, it will take human technology to the next level. 'People have tried hard and a Nobel Prize is guaranteed for anybody who discovers superconductivity at room temperature,' says Archana.

Watch out, she might just win the next Nobel Prize for Physics! Or perhaps, it will be you?

GAGANDEEP
KANG
Clinical scientist

Gagandeep was a clinician-doctor, who moved into research so she can save even more lives. As an epidemiologist, she played a big role in testing the rotavirus vaccine that is set to save millions of lives around the world.

KEEPING INDIA'S GUTS HEALTHY

Amidst the throng of elderly men who lead Indian science, very few women are visible. Gagandeep's calm smiling face is one of them. In her thirty years of work on India's public health, Gagandeep has emerged at the top, thanks to her extraordinary intelligence.

One day, when Gagandeep was eight years old, she received news of the death of the newborn baby of her neighbourhood washerwoman in Jamalpur, Bihar. A few days before this, the young Gagandeep had asked the washerwoman about the knotted red thread that she wore around her wrist. The washerwoman had told her that her baby was sick and the thread was from a healer who had promised her that when the knots loosened, her baby would recover. A few days later, Gagandeep heard loud wailing and her mother told her that the washerwoman's baby had died. They had not gone to a doctor. Instead they had gone to a traditional healer in the belief that faith alone would heal the baby. 'That was when I decided that I would help people in India change their way of getting medical treatment,' says Gagandeep.

Gagandeep started out as a doctor of medicine and only later became a scientist. She was seeing many patients a day as a doctor but soon became impatient with the routine. At a lecture one day, she heard another doctor say: 'In my lifetime I can see 1,00,000 patients, but if I discover a new drug, I will be treating millions of patients.' Inspired by this idea, she decided to dedicate her life to researching diseases in India.

Today, Gagandeep is consulted on many matters with regard to India's public health. She understands the Indian gut, or intestines, more than anyone else in the world. If you ask her, she will tell you all about the Indian gut. From the parasites that infect it to the good microorganisms that are part of our digestion—she has studied them all.

For the last thirty years, Gagandeep has been investigating the gut health of a large group that is now 1,50,000 strong. She has found that Indians are exposed to gut infections very early on in their lives. Infectious parasites are all around us, but we don't get sick from them as often as you would expect. The Indian gut, Gagandeep has discovered, adapts very quickly to infections. 'We carry around disease-causing parasites quite comfortably without necessarily contracting diseases,' she says.

This might sound like a good thing, but in fact it is very worrying. Our ability to live with many parasites results in repeated inflammation in our guts. It also reduces our guts' ability to absorb nutrients from food. This means that the nutrients that we eat cannot be used by the body—they are wasted. India has very high rates of malnutrition and understanding how the gut works is crucial in solving this huge problem.

This parasite-caused inflammation of the gut also makes vaccines ineffective on Indian bodies, specifically those vaccines that are taken orally and not injected. According to Gagandeep's research, vaccines for diarrhoea-causing rotavirus as well as the polio virus are not as effective in Indians as they are in other populations. This discovery is her major contribution to Indian science. The steps she took after discovering this will save the lives of millions.

After identifying the problem of ineffective vaccines, Gagandeep took up the challenge of working on new vaccines for Indians. Her team tested a new vaccine for rotavirus. It was approved by the Indian government in 2016 and is now being distributed throughout the country. She has also worked with Indian vaccine manufacturers to prepare and test various other vaccines. Along with the Indian government, she is tracking how these vaccines are working. Her success in this field has taken her to Brazil and China, where she has helped in testing new vaccines for their populations.

Gagandeep continues her work with the Indian government to find out how vaccines work on the Indian gut. Her team of 250 scientific staff, has tested most major vaccines that are used in the country today.

Infectious diseases aside, Gagandeep has become concerned about the rise of non-communicable diseases like diabetes and heart problems in the Indian population. These are usually linked to lifestyle choices. She strongly advises the Indian government to do more to tackle these public health nightmares. Improving the health of the country cannot be left in the hands of private companies, she believes. There is a lot more at stake than profit making. 'We need to approach the patient as a person and not as a disease,' she always says.

JAHNAVI
PUNEKAR
Palaeontologist

Jahnavi, a palaeontologist, is a Jurassic Park fan who studies microscopic seashells to explain climate change events that have taken place on the planet.

A Time-lapse of Life on Earth

Jurassic Park was nine-year-old Jahnavi's favourite film. Every time she watched it, she saw herself as one of the scientists who studied dinosaurs. She wanted it all—the brushes, the khaki jacket, the hammers, maps and a caravan full of dino fossils. By the time she was ten, Jahnavi had declared that she would grow up to be a palaeontologist. She spent her time learning about the evolution of life on earth though books, movies and more. Jahnavi's parents didn't pressure her to be a doctor or an engineer. She was free to choose what she wanted to study. She chose geology—the study of the layers of the earth, within which she would find the remains of dinosaurs and other creatures.

'Making a career decision at ten and being taken seriously by your parents comes with a strange kind of responsibility—a drive to make it happen and earn their and your own faith in yourself,' she says. This drive got her to the point, after college, when she could commit fully to her childhood dream.

Palaeontology is a branch of geology that involves the study of fossils—the dead remains of things that once lived. Fossils, found preserved in sedimentary rocks, are important tools for studying the progression of life on earth. Older layers are deposited first, while younger sediments are layered on top of the older ones. Jahnavi likes to imagine that these layers are like the pages of a book.

She reads the layers like a book to recreate the history of earth—its climate and geography. In this metaphorical 'book' of geological time, the 'pages' are the layers of the earth and the 'words' are the fossils found in them. The 'chapters' of the book are separated by major events in earth's life story, like the mass extinction of species that often goes hand in hand with dramatic climate change on the planet.

Our earth is 4.5 billion years old and the oldest fossils found are from 4 billion years ago. Big dinosaurs roamed the earth between 250 million years to 66 million years ago. Jahnavi is focused on the layers of the earth from an era called the Cretaceous period, which runs from 175 million years ago to 66 million years ago. The end of the Cretaceous period is especially interesting to her as it marks the demise of the big dinosaurs. What killed so many dinosaurs? Was it the impact of a big meteorite crashing into earth as is popularly believed or was it a ginormous volcanic event that occurred around the same time? Jahnavi is trying to find out.

Ironically, Jahnavi does not study large dinosaur fossils as they are rare to find. Instead, she works with the tiny microscopic shells of marine animals called foraminifera. These shells are abundant in ocean sediments even today. And these animals come in beautiful shapes; some even look like popcorn under a microscope!

When alive, these tiny animals are very sensitive—minor changes in their environment are reflected in them through changes in their size, shape, abundance and diversity. Jahnavi investigates the ups and downs in foraminifera population sizes to determine the conditions on the planet when they lived. Life on earth responds to climate change very quickly; Jahnavi knows this scientific fact very well. For example, when the population size of these popcorn creatures in ocean sediments is reduced drastically, Jahnavi takes it as a sign of dramatic change in the environment.

Jahnavi aims to make a layer-by-layer time-lapse of the environmental or climatic changes of the critical Cretaceous period that ended in the dramatic mass extinction of many species of tiny foraminifera as well as all of the big dinosaurs.

Along with her research partners, she is putting forward a theory that this mass extinction may be related to the catastrophic series of Deccan volcanic eruptions that also took place 66 million years ago. These volcanos spilled lava on and created a large part of what we now call India. It resulted in the basaltic terrain of western, southern and central India and gave rise to the magnificent Western Ghats. It is considered to be one of the largest volcanic events in the history of our planet. It caused a rapid release of copious amounts of carbon dioxide, sulphur dioxide and other toxic gases. Jahnavi's theory suggests that these gases might have caused major global climatic changes that most life forms of that time could not survive.

Today, as we face climate change caused by human activities, research like Jahnavi's is very important. It can help us predict the future of life on earth by making comparisons with similar events of the past. Jahnavi has some advice for young people who might be confused about what to study further: 'You do your best when you do what you really like! If you can figure out that one thing that you can forget your hunger and sleep for, you probably have an idea of what to turn into your work.'

UMA
RAMAKRISHNAN
Molecular ecologist

Uma is on a mission to save the Indian tiger from extinction. She has new molecular techniques up her sleeve, to keep a check on the genetic diversity of tiger species in our national parks.

A Genetic Eye on the Tiger

Many of Uma's childhood days were spent in the home of a friend whose father was an ecologist. She found his work in nature conservation fascinating. With her parents, she travelled to national parks where she saw that nature was wondrous and beautiful but it was also mysterious. Why do elephants have trunks and why are goats great at climbing mountains? These were fascinating mysteries to the young Uma. 'Finding out the *why*s in nature felt like detective work,' Uma says.

Very early on, she realized her favourite subject—ecology—could be studied as a quantitative science with numbers, equations and graphs. In college, she studied maths, chemistry and physics instead of biology, even though she was sure she wanted to be an ecologist.

Uma went to America to start her research life. But returning to India was pre-decided. 'I am connected to this land! There was no other option but to come back.' Her connection to the land is rooted in her love for India's wildlife and the animal that is most dear to her—the tiger—is found most commonly in India.

Big wild cats like tigers, leopards and lions are very territorial animals. Each rules over a large area of a forest, marking it with chemical signals in their pee and poop to express warning, love and other kinds of messages. As humans take up more and more space, the habitats of these wonderful animals are shrinking. Saving endangered animals is a national priority. This requires maintaining a healthy, connected population of these animals.

Today a molecular ecologist working in Bengaluru, Uma leads the scientific-minded bandwagon to save the Indian tiger from extinction. She is a special kind of conservation ecologist. Instead of spotting the animals with hidden cameras, she analyses the genetics of the animals from their poop and hair. With this technique, she has estimated the number of Indian tigers in some protected forests and is able to advice forest officials on how to save the tiger.

'As scientists in India, if we do not have genetic information on a species that is so much in the public imagination, what are we doing? It is our responsibility to create good data, to understand the species better. I feel I must take on this responsibility,' she says.

In the field, Uma and her team trek along forest trails collecting tiger poop and hair. These samples are then taken to their lab where most of the work happens. The tiger DNA is extracted and a genetic profile is created for each tiger. Parts of the DNA called SNP loci help to make a profile that is unique to every individual animal. Tigers that are related have similar genetic profiles. A healthy large population of tigers, free of the threat of extinction, needs to have the maximum diversity of genetic profiles, that is, as many different types as possible. Uma has been busy predicting if tiger populations will continue to be genetically diverse despite the roads and cities we are building. She found out a lot about tiger populations in this process. Her success in putting together accurate tiger counts is proof that genetics is an important tool for wildlife protection.

Uma's method not only helps to keep a count of India's tigers year after year, it also helps in studying their genetic diversity. With her molecular analysis, she has identified healthy, genetically diverse tiger populations that live in connected habitats and also some groups with low genetic diversity in isolated pockets that face the threat of being wiped out.

As the human population increases, wild animals are being cornered into smaller and smaller areas. Connectivity between parks where tigers live is crucial to keep the genetic diversity of the population healthy. The genetic diversity of a species is a marker of its ability to survive threats of extinction. Low genetic diversity decreases the chances of the population surviving. This is the direct effect of inbreeding, that is, animals breeding within their own family or within small populations.

Inbreeding causes lower reproduction rates and allows disease to spread faster, thereby hastening decrease in population.

Uma's studies have found that the total genetic diversity of all Indian tigers together has reduced drastically but it is still higher than anywhere else in the world. She knows that India's tigers are at risk. There are many small pockets of different tigers around the country but these pockets are not connected. She also found that individual genomes of Indian tigers show signs of inbreeding, which should be prevented as much as possible to make tiger populations thrive. This is why Uma firmly campaigns for wildlife corridors through which animals can move around freely across protected areas.

Uma's investigations into the genetic diversity of populations allow the police to identify the geographic origins of illegal leopard skins. Her genetic work on connectivity was also used to legally argue for and win a case on animal passage in the Supreme Court of India. This led to the building of the biggest underpass in the world under National Highway 7, which bisects the Kanha-Pench wildlife reserve in central India.

Because of the efforts of conservation scientists like Uma, as well as activists and forest officers, the number of tigers in India is increasing.

RICHA
RIKHY
Cell biologist

Richa cares for and breeds fruit flies in her Fly Lab. In return, the flies reveal to her, under her powerful microscopes, the amazing changes that we all went through when we started our life from a single round cell.

MAKING ART WITH FRUIT FLIES

Ten-year-old Richa loved to draw. She drew people, trees, plants and animals. But most of all, she drew little circles with dots in them. These were cells. She had been fascinated by them ever since she'd heard from her mother and father that she herself was once a single cell.

We all start off as single cells inside our mother's wombs. That single cell, called the zygote, grows into a multicellular embryo, which then develops into the magnificent multicellular organism that we are. The transformation from zygote to a multicellular embryo is a wonderful step-by-step process that occurs naturally. This process is similar in all animal embryos, whether it is a human or a fruit fly. Richa likes to observe these initial stages of life in fruit fly zygotes.

Richa grew up to be a cell biologist, but you can also think of her as an artist and a filmmaker. In her lab, she has several high-power microscopes with which she makes films of a single cell dividing to become an embryo. These images are still very artistic and awe-inspiring for Richa. But she knows that these films are so much more. By recording the first steps of life, Richa is able to make many scientific discoveries about the changes that happen at the cellular level to make us a complete organism.

'Microscopy attracted me very early on. It fits right in with my interests in drawing and painting and architecture. Sometimes, I feel my science is the way it is because I like art so much,' she says.

Since studying human embryos is difficult and is considered ethically problematic, Richa uses fruit fly embryos. Through millions of years of evolution, the architecture of the developing organism has remained somewhat unchanged. This is why discoveries made by looking at how fruit flies' embryos develop are helpful to understand human development. Fruit flies are also very small and easy to handle. They have a lifespan of only forty to fifty days, so they live and die very fast. This short life cycle is very useful if you want to study developmental biology like Richa does.

In fact, Richa has set up a fruit fly lab at her institute in Pune with her colleagues. Thousands of flies live, feed, breed and are taken care of by Richa and her team in this lab. Fruit fly zygotes are carried from here to another lab that has many high-power microscopes. In the microscope lab, Richa makes beautiful films of all the changes that happen at the beginning of a fruit fly's life.

Richa first inserts a gene into the single cell or zygote she wants to study. This gene has the special power of making some parts of the cell glow. Then she takes the glowing zygote to the microscope. Under the microscope, one part of the zygote shines fluorescent. Let's say this glowing part of the cell is the glow of the plasma membrane—the outer boundary or the cover of the cell.

As the cell divides and embryo forms, Richa observes the changes in the plasma membranes as they go from being simple to complex. At various microscopic powers, there are many discoveries to be made. Richa records embryos developing in four dimensions—length, breadth, width and time. In just two hours, the outer layer of the fruit fly embryo goes from one cell to 6,000 cells. From one round cell, it becomes a rectangular sheet of thousands of cells. Then the cells become polygonal with many sides and then turn into a ball-like embryo. Some specific molecules help cells achieve all these shapes. And Richa observes all of this.

There are many mysteries about the architecture of the embryo that have remained unanswered. Richa is a biologist inspired by art, who is looking for these answers with the help of powerful microscopes. She looks at cells much like you may look at the room you are sitting in: what makes the cell, what are the features of the cell and how does one cell of a particular shape and size give rise to different cells with different jobs.

Richa experiments by manipulating different fruit fly genes to find what mechanisms are involved in embryonic development. For example, her research question might be something like 'if I disturb the genetic coding for the organization of the plasma membrane, does the embryo become floppy and unable to maintain its shape and therefore the activities inside'?

'Art is a motivation for my approach in biology,' says Richa. If being a scientist had not worked out, Richa thinks she would be making animated movies!

12

RAMA GOVINDARAJAN

Fluid dynamicist

An expert in fluid dynamics, Rama writes equations to unravel the workings of a yearly miracle that affects the lives of more than a billion people—the Indian monsoon.

Decoding the Indian Monsoon

Sometimes, it takes some more than a little grit and courage to do what you believe in. Rama Govindarajan learnt this early on. As a child growing up in the cities of Delhi and Chennai, she was always inspired by the story of how her grandmother stood up to her own community by eating in the home of a family from a backward caste, which was considered taboo. And then there was her brave mother, who raised Rama by herself and made sure that there was never any shortage of laughter and art in her life, even when times were tough.

While studying chemical engineering in college, Rama was the only girl among fifty-four students. Coming from an all-girls school, this was a totally new atmosphere for her. But Rama knew that her gender would not matter as long as she was good at what she did. And she was. Rama was always the best student in class, and she also made many close friends on the way.

A full-fledged engineer, Rama did not think of becoming a scientist until many years later. She got a job that paid her well and looked set to lead a comfortable life like most of her friends. However, two months into her job, Rama realized that something was missing. She was longing for something more challenging and meaningful, even if it meant a less luxurious lifestyle. It took her many more years of studying and training to realize that the field she was meant to be in was scientific research.

Rama specializes in an area of engineering and physics called fluid dynamics. Today, at her centre in Bengaluru, she and her colleagues are hard at work, trying to uncover the secrets behind a yearly miracle that affects the lives of more than a billion people. This phenomenon unfolds every year between June and September. It is the biggest weather system in the world—the Indian monsoon. Despite our lives depending on the monsoon, we still do not clearly know what sets off the rainy season so suddenly and dramatically in our country.

Did you know that India usually receives about the same quantity of rainfall every year? Severe droughts and floods are a result of just slight deviations from the average. Even a bad year gives us almost ninety per cent of the average rainfall. But a ten to twenty per cent variation is more than enough to wreak havoc on the whole nation. Agricultural yields are affected badly, which leads to food shortages. Wells and lakes dry up, and floods that destroy lives and livelihoods can also occur.

Scientists like Rama use statistical methods to find patterns in the rainfall. Statistics is the study of patterns in large quantities of numerical data—in this case, weather data. Weather data from satellites make her patterns more accurate. Rama hopes that one day, her work can be used to make predictive models, using which farmers would be able to plan their activities better; economists would be able to brace the markets for difficult times ahead; and the general public would be more mindful about their water consumption. However, even with advanced computational power, Rama is aware that it would take more than a hundred years before scientists could build an exact model of the Indian monsoon. So, she started small, by studying the behaviour of one of the most fundamental units of the monsoon—the cloud.

Rama has been trying to understand clouds for years now. Her fascination with clouds began while she was doing research in aerospace engineering. One day, she witnessed her advisor, an aerospace scientist, conducting a very interesting experiment. Using water, he had created a coloured 'cloud' in his laboratory. His model cloud would rise up to unexpected heights, just like a real one. When Rama saw the swirling vortexes in this coloured cloud of water, she was transfixed. Who imagined that there was so much going on inside those fluffy clouds in the sky?

Rama has her eyes on how clouds form and move because this is what influences their rain-making ability. She writes equations to describe how water vapour rises from earth's surface and forms rain clouds in the air. The equations in her model look a little more complicated than 'x + y = z' because they involve many more variables such as space, time, velocity, temperature, rainfall, density, moisture content and salinity of the ocean.

Climatic models exist for the world as a whole, but the Indian monsoon is a unique case. Every year, there are big gaps between what is predicted and what actually happens. If Rama and rest of India's monsoon scientists succeed in creating the model, it would mean the dawn of a new and more secure future for the whole country.

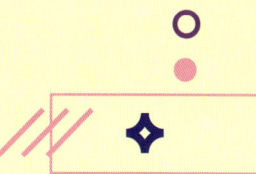

13

ARUNA
NAOREM
Molecular geneticist

Dicty cells are tiny, hungry and very smart team-players. They are Aruna's favourite microorganisms. She spends her days experimenting with them to understand the genes that make them special.

THRIVING IN DIFFICULT ENVIRONMENTS

Aruna was born in the state of Manipur in a small town called Kakching. When she was fifteen-years-old, she had to leave her parents and live with her uncle in the city because the schools there were bigger and better than the ones in Kakching. However, even in the city, she soon found that things were far from ideal. The whole state of Manipur was suffering from political instability and there were frequent bursts of violence that endangered people's lives. As a matter of fact, one of the most unforgettable experiences of Aruna's life was a march she participated in. It was a silent march for justice for her state and it was on her very first day in the twelfth standard. When it was time to go to college, Aruna was one of the many students from Manipur to move out of their home state to safer places. She packed her bags and went to Delhi.

Having topped the biology exam in school, Aruna felt herself falling further in love with the subject in college. Indeed, biology came to be her true calling. Always too restless to stay seated on a bench in front of a book or a computer, Aruna looked for every opportunity to jump up and do experiments. Genetics is a field in biology that involves a lot of lab experiments! So she decided to get trained in genetics and for this, she travelled to the best laboratories in India.

Each place Aruna moved to was considerably different from the previous one, so she had to make lots of adjustments. Delhi was much bigger and noisier than Manipur. And in Kerala, she was surprised to see that the rice was so much bigger and not sticky and white like the kind she was used to at home. Aruna adapted to her surroundings and went deeper into understanding genetics.

While she was doing her PhD, a degree that starts off most scientists' careers, Aruna encountered a special type of soil microorganism called *Dictyostelium discoideum,* nicknamed Dicty. These single-cell microbes have something in common with Aruna: they too are very good at adapting to difficult situations. Though they are made up of just one cell, Dicty cells are great team players. They *love* to eat and are really good at sniffing their way to food. In nature, these creatures are really common, especially in soil. In her lab, Aruna grows them on special plates, flasks or tubes.

When they're hungry—and that's a lot of the time—Dicty cells can sense when food is nearby and crawl towards it. In her lab, Aruna has a microscope by her side so she can watch her cells sniff around. Sometimes, she removes the food and tests what happens. When there is no food around, Dicty cells don't panic—they have a plan to avoid starvation. They begin to team up and huddle together in a shape called a fruiting body. This is when things start to get interesting for Aruna as a scientist. Dicty fruiting bodies can tell us a lot about how we humans came to be the complex living creatures that we are.

Remember, you did not always look the way you do now. Each of us started out as a single cell inside our mother's womb. This single cell multiplied into many cells and then they began taking up special duties. Some became blood cells, some brain cells and so on. How does a human cell decide what it will become? That's a question difficult enough to make even a scientist dizzy.

Enter Dicty cells. While humans have hundreds of types of cells, the Dicty fruiting body has only two types of cells. The ones on top turn into small hard spores, waiting till new food turns up. These spores can then grow into new Dicty cells keeping their family tree alive. Underneath the live spores is a stalk, made up of dead cells. These cells have sacrificed themselves so that their spore friends can live on. Saving and sharing available energy is their best bet to survive these times of starvation.

These days, Aruna spends her time in her laboratory at the University of Delhi, working towards her mission of understanding how a Dicty cell decides which duty to take up. Which of their genes are responsible for making this decision: should they live on as spores or should they sacrifice themselves? Being a geneticist, her strategy is to play with their genes. Each discovery she makes about the working of the Dicty cell brings us closer to understanding how complicated creatures like humans work. Piece by piece, Aruna and other scientists like her are solving the puzzles of life.

SUDHA
AGRAHARI
Hydro geophysicist

Everyone needs water to survive, but clean water is a precious and rare resource for a lot of people in the world. With her special machines, Sudha measures the electrical properties of water to find, map and make clean water available to these people.

A Geophysicist and Her Water Bots

Sudha grew up in Gorakhpur, Uttar Pradesh, in a family that was supported by her father who worked as a railway serviceman. She was the brightest student in her school. She loved physics but there were not many good schools around that could have helped her take her interest forward. 'I want to do science that impacts people's lives directly,' she told her teachers at school. Thanks to her teachers' encouragement to pursue her dreams, she pushed on and reached further and further, until she finally made it as a scientist.

'I didn't study in big schools—but my teachers always wanted me to go to better schools. And somehow I kept getting scholarships and fellowships to support my studies. One thing was very clear to me—I will pursue science, come what may,' Sudha said.

Today, Sudha is a water scientist. To protect our groundwater from being overused and polluted, we need geophysicists like her. Large amounts of water flow underground. Earth's layers act as a natural filter to store clean groundwater in aquifers. She specializes in mapping aquifers—the underground pockets where groundwater collects. Sudha uses the laws of physics to detect the precise locations of these aquifers.

For daily use and consumption, borewells are dug, which connect aquifers to the surface. Almost all communities in India are dependent on groundwater for their water supply. In fact, satellites have detected that north India is overusing groundwater for agricultural purposes. We are using up all the water before rain and natural water currents can replenish it. And, every year, there are more reports of the groundwater being contaminated with dyes, pesticides and other chemicals harmful to our health.

A special technique called ERT—electrical resistivity tomography—helps Sudha know what lies underneath without any digging. ERT measures the electric resistivity of the groundwater using four to forty-two electric rods inserted into the ground. With this simple machine, she can also tell how big the aquifers are and whether they are connected to other aquifers.

Sudha has worked in coastal areas, where fresh clean groundwater can get contaminated with seawater, or worse, with industrial waste that has been released into the sea. She has also mapped groundwater in the Himalayas. This was very tricky, since groundwater in mountainous ranges have a tendency to disappear for some months of the year. There are other problems too. 'The Himalayas are one of the toughest terrains to do fieldwork in. You have to go everywhere by foot and carry huge equipment up and down the mountains all the time. We had to return several times because the terrain was too difficult to work in.'

To get around this problem, Sudha went to Germany to study airborne electromagnetic methods. In these methods, helicopters and drones are loaded with a piece of advanced electromagnetic equipment that allows the analysis of the sub-surface without any contact. As a matter of fact, the instrument may be hovering approximately 10–100 metres above the land. Sudha is one of the very few experts in the country working with this technique.

Earth's subsurface is not uniformly resistive. Resistivity is the property that quantifies how strongly a given material opposes the flow of electric current. Low resistivity indicates a material that readily allows the flow of electric current through it. The current has to put more effort to cross a highly resistive material, leading to an electric potential drop, which is then recorded.

Assessing resistivity with ERT to find out whether water is drinkable or not is a really smart idea. Most contaminating agents in water are conductive in nature, meaning they have low resistivity. Canned water has a resistivity of 50–70 ohm-metres. In Sudha's experience, groundwater with a resistivity of 50–90 ohm-metres is suitable for drinking, but 'of course there are also other aspects that should also be taken into consideration to make sure', she cautions.

These kinds of studies are tremendously useful, especially in the absence of proper plumbing and water pipelines in our country's remote towns and villages. When borewells or handpumps are dug, it is crucial to take ERT measurements. An expert is needed in case a well runs dry and another borewell is needed or to determine whether or not the water source is contaminated. Sudha is happy to be this person. She loves her work.

'It's very interesting to see that a farmer who has had no education in his life has made a groundwater recharge system, just out of his experience and his need. I learn so much on the field. Here, you are no longer merely a part of the science community. You get to know about the real requirements of the common people. It is fascinating,' Sudha says.

KANEENIKA
SINHA
Number theorist }

During a maths camp, Kaneenika fell in love with the subject in a way she had never expected. Mathematics was no longer just a subject to score marks in, but a world of fun and challenges. Today, she spends her life in this world.

FALLING IN LOVE AT MATHS CAMP

As the daughter of an army officer, Kaneenika spent her childhood moving and living in several parts of India. Her parents had great dreams for her. They thought she should prepare for the incredibly competitive civil services exams and secure a respectable government job. Before she could qualify for this examination, Kaneenika would need to complete a course in college. It could have been any course, but she chose mathematics because she found it easy to score high marks in the subject. However, during a maths camp, she fell in love with the subject in a way she had never expected. Mathematics was no longer just a subject to score marks in, but a world of fun and challenges. Kaneenika decided that she wanted to spend her life inside this world.

As a mathematician, Kaneenika spends her time reading, writing and solving several problems. Today, she is also a teacher to students who dream of becoming mathematicians themselves. One day, Kaneenika put forth a challenge to her students. She told them to start at the first prime number—2—and on each day from then on, solve as many problems as it takes to reach the next prime number. 'That's easy', said her students. And indeed, for the first few days, it was easy.

On day 0, they only had to solve 2 problems, as the first prime is 2.
On day 1, 1 problem to get to the next prime 3 (3–2=1)
On day 2, 2 problems to get to 5 (5–3=2)
On day 3, 2 problems to get to 7 (7–5=2)
On day 4, 4 problems to get to 11 (11–7=4)
And on day 5, 2 problems since 13 is the next prime. (13–7=5)

Day 30 was a bit challenging for some students because they had to solve 14 problems (127–113=14). But things stabilized after that, and for months, the students did not have to solve more than 20 problems a day. Then came day 217, when they had to solve 34 problems!

Her students could go on forever because prime numbers, although they become rarer and rarer as we go further in the number series, never stop popping up. Do they follow any pattern or are prime numbers distributed completely randomly? This is something that has puzzled mathematicians like Kaneenika for centuries. Studying the distributions of numbers and searching for patterns is what number theory is about and this is what Kaneenika specializes in.

One of the most famous mysteries of number theory is called the 'twin prime conjecture'. According to this, there should be an infinite number of twin primes—prime numbers separated by 2, such as 3 and 5, 11 and 13, 41 and 43. That means if Kaneenika's students continue their challenge forever, there will always be days on which they solve only 2 problems. The conjecture does seem to be true—mathematicians have calculated twin primes that are 3,88,342 digits long! Still, a 'conjecture' isn't the truth unless a mathematician is able to come up with definitive proof, but that day has not come yet.

Kaneenika loves the challenges that numbers throw up and this is what made her study mathematics. She found she was really good at it, too! Today, she is studying the distribution of other special numbers called Fourier coefficients. She was trained by several mathematicians in Canada before she returned to India to join a team of number theorists in one of the country's top research institutes. The corridors in her department are lined with green boards for Kaneenika and her mathematician friends to scribble calculations on. After all, you never know when an idea will strike!

Though maths is fundamental to many human activities like engineering and technology, Kaneenika is most enamoured by mathematics of the pure kind. The pure sciences and mathematics are full of theories and may seem very abstract. However, they explore such deep questions about the universe that they cannot be ignored. They are never performed with an application in mind, nevertheless, some of the greatest inventions in human history are based on pure science and maths discoveries. For example, prime numbers form the foundation of encryption methods which need to be used today to make our online experiences such as shopping and banking secure. Without it, we would not be able to carry out important tasks on the Internet.

Working in number theory continues to hold the same thrill for Kaneenika as it did when she was a college student at maths camp. Who knew mathematics held the key to so many age-old mysteries and unimaginable promises for the future!

VIDITA
VAIDYA
Neuroscientist

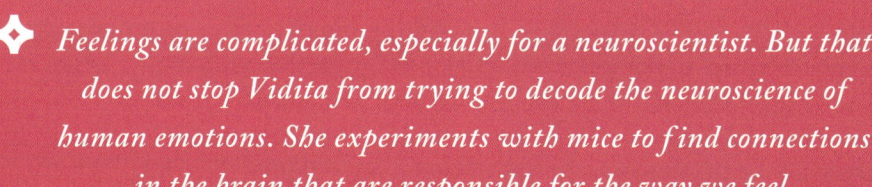

Feelings are complicated, especially for a neuroscientist. But that does not stop Vidita from trying to decode the neuroscience of human emotions. She experiments with mice to find connections in the brain that are responsible for the way we feel.

Reading the Brain's Mind

Four-year-old Vidita watched the caterpillar sway in the wind, dangling on the thread that it had woven. The caterpillar would soon wrap the silken threads around its body to build itself a nice comfortable cocoon. As she gazed at the busy little creature, she wondered, *how does the caterpillar know how long the thread has to be to make the perfect home*?

Over the years, Vidita came to realize that all the decisions that animals make come from their brains. Even the most basic action, such as looking at this book, is controlled by your brain. Your eyes are seeing the colours and words on this page. Light signals from your eyes are converted into electric signals, which travel across your nerves to your brain. Your brain then converts the visual information into actual images. So it may look like it is the eyes that see, but it's actually the brain that is doing the actual 'seeing'. Similarly, it is the brain that 'smells', 'hears', 'speaks', and 'feels' too.

When she realized the amazing powers of the brain, Vidita decided that she would spend her life solving its mysteries. Her parents—both doctors—inspired her to follow her dreams. It's not easy to become a brain scientist, but Vidita was ready to work really hard for it. And it paid off! Vidita was able to study at the top universities in North America and Europe to train to become a scientist. Working under international experts in neuroscience, she quickly grasped the tricks of the trade. Years later, at twenty-nine years of age, she returned to her homeland to set up her very own neuroscience laboratory in Mumbai. Her lab is a scenic research institution on the shores of the Arabian Sea. Together with a team of dedicated younger scientists, Vidita is trying to decode the neuroscience of emotions.

Our feelings are a complicated business. And this is exactly what makes humans so special. Behind all of the joy we feel, the tears that fall and the drama we experience is the brain. The brain is made up of cells called neurons, which are connected to each other so that information can travel from one end to another. It's like a giant network of circuits. But what's fascinating is that this network is not fixed. Every day, there are minor tweaks being made. New contacts between neurons are created and previously linked neurons that are not in use are disconnected. Vidita calls this quality of the brain plasticity. Just like plastic can be melted and moulded into different shapes, the brain's neurons connect and disconnect as we go through life. It's not easy to study something that is constantly changing, but like any good scientist, Vidita loves a good challenge.

She is trying to figure out which connections in the brain are responsible for the way we feel. Which brain connections are activated when you're happy or jealous or stressed? Why do identical twins sometimes react differently to the same situations? Why do medicines for depression work for some people and not work for some others? To answer any of these questions, Vidita needs to perform experiments.

Of course, Vidita can't just pick people off the street and play with their feelings. That's not right. So, she turns to animals. Mice are most neuroscientists' favourite animals. They have a short life span, reproduce faster than humans and their brains are quite easy to observe. After years and years of experimenting on mice, Vidita noticed something scary: the brains of stressed-out baby mice grew older much quicker than the brains of mice with happier childhoods. This means that traumatic and stressful experiences—due to starvation, an accident, abandonment or any other reason—that occur during their childhood can affect their brains and health later in life. Vidita is pretty sure that this is true in human beings too.

The good news is that a young person's brain is much more 'plastic' than an older brain. So, if children who have gone through some kind of trauma are given the right kind of attention early, Vidita is confident that their brain can 'fix' itself before the damage becomes irreversible.

Very few other scientists are doing research on the brain and emotions in India, so Vidita's work is quite special. In 2015, the country recognized this by awarding her its biggest science award, the Shanti Swarup Bhatnagar Prize in the medical sciences category. Just like the caterpillar's thread, Vidita is busy in her lab spinning threads of research, waiting for the day when all science can be wound together to tell us everything we need to know about the brain.

JIS
SEBASTIAN
Conservation ecologist

Jis is a conservation ecologist who has dedicated her life to studying threats to the environment and coming up with ways to address them. After years of studying bears, gibbons, orchids and butterflies, the Indian wilderness feels just like home to her.

Journeying in the Wilderness

Every evening, the young Jis Sebastian would walk along the paddy fields of Kudakkachira, her village in Kerala, among wild trees and sparkling streams. Over time, something began to worry her. The number of trees was reducing drastically. 'Why are the trees being chopped down?' she asked the people around her. 'Isn't it useful to have them around?'

She was dissatisfied with their answers and determined to find out for herself all about the danger our environment is in. She did not mind leaving home for this purpose. And to that end, twenty-year-old Jis took her first ever train ride. It was a long one. She headed to hilly Dehradun—almost 3,000 km away—to study ecology. Today, she is a conservation ecologist. She has dedicated her life to studying threats to the environment and coming up with ways to address them.

Jis's first wildlife project was to observe the Asiatic black bears of the Himalayas. Asiatic black bears are one of four bear species that live in India. They are big black bears with crescent-shaped white marks on their chests. They are powerful climbers and spend much of their time up in trees. But these powerful creatures are in trouble.

Along with the forest cover of the Himalayas, the population of Asiatic black bears is shrinking. Forests, where these wild bears live, are being cleared for human use and the bears no longer have enough space to live. They have begun to stray into towns and villages in search of space and food, damaging agricultural land in the process. The local people are greatly affected by an increasing number of such instances, and are unsure of how they can put a stop to them. Many times, people react to such human-animal conflicts by killing animals. Besides this, the bears are also hunted by poachers for their bile—the fluid inside their livers—which is believed to cure several diseases. It's no wonder then, that there is an urgent need to conserve the Asiatic black bear. This is why Jis was sent to Kashmir's Dachigam National Park.

At the park, Jis had to find out exactly where the bears lived. Asiatic black bears eat mostly plants, so she chose to arrive at the park during springtime. In the fruit-filled orchards of the national park, Jis waited and watched. Sure enough after a while, there descended the hungry bears! For four months, Jis tracked the bears—paw prints, dung, everything was a clue! She took notes on everything she saw. What kind of plants were they eating? How often were they eating? Where were their favourite places to hang out and why? She knew that any new information could be crucial towards building a strategy to boost the population of this vulnerable species.

For her next project, Jis went to Arunachal Pradesh. She had to cross the Brahmaputra River to get to a remote village in Dibang Valley situated at the easternmost part of India. She lived with the native people there for more than a year. Jis was there for a very specific reason—to study the hoolock gibbon, the only apes that live in India, besides humans.

Hoolock gibbons have long arms and short legs. These make them rather clumsy on the ground but more comfortable on trees. Like Asiatic black bears, the hoolock population is on the decline as well. In Dibang Valley, where Jis lived, more and more trees were being cut down to clear the land for agriculture, so the hoolocks were losing their homes. Forest officials decided that the hoolock families needed to be relocated from the village to a nearby sanctuary, where there were many more trees.

How would one go about capturing so many hoolocks? It was Jis's job to answer this question and make sure the relocation was smooth. From sunrise to sunset, she would crouch near the hoolocks, observing them and taking notes. Over the year, the hoolocks allowed her to come closer and closer. Eventually, they began to recognize her as one of their own!

Jis's passion for the wilderness grew and grew. After her adventures with the bears and apes, she went to Assam to study butterflies, and then back to south India to study orchids in the Western Ghats. She has also run campaigns to raise awareness about sustainable tourism and eco-friendly menstruation. She conducts campaigns to encourage local communities and panchayats to participate in the conservation of their own environments. Impressed by her work in nature conservation, the World Wildlife Fund (WWF) gave her a prestigious scholarship in 2017. Such awards help her accomplish even more in her conservation efforts in India.

A lot of Jis's work as a conservation ecologist sees her travelling to remote places for long periods of time. She has to climb trees, hide behind bushes and go on long mountain treks, often with no humans for company. But Jis never feels alone in the wild—not with her plant and animal friends. She feels safe, happy and as free as the wind. No wonder she's determined to save the forests.

DEVAPRIYA
CHATTOPADHYAY
Palaeobiologist

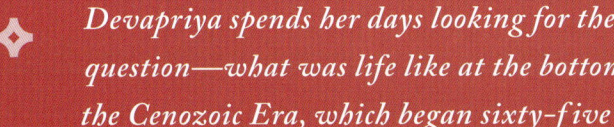

Devapriya spends her days looking for the answer to one big question—what was life like at the bottom of the sea during the Cenozoic Era, which began sixty-five million years ago? For this, she has to travel back in time. She does that not with a time machine, but with fossils!

TIME TRAVELLING WITH FOSSILS

While growing up, Devapriya often followed her father into the forests near their home in north Bengal. While he painted landscapes, Devapriya would stroll around, observing nature at play. So much was going on with the rocks, trees and insects around her. *How did all this come to be*? she wondered. She had so many questions about the history of the earth that she decided to become a scientist who could discover some of the answers. She became a palaeobiologist.

Devapriya spends her days looking for the answer to one big question—what was life like on the sea floor during the Cenozoic Era, which began sixty-five million years ago? At this time, non-avian dinosaurs had just become extinct. What was once a single mass of land surrounded by a vast ocean drifted apart to form the seven continents we know today. The Indian subcontinent was on its northward move and had just crossed the equator. In another thirty million years or so, it would collide with Asia, giving rise to the gigantic Himalayan mountain ranges. The Tethys Ocean that used to occupy this space would then close up. In the later part of the Cenozoic Era—the Miocene—the Tethys would disconnect from its western arm to form what is now the Arabian Sea. One of the things that Devapriya does is study the effect that this change had on the sea creatures of that time.

To study what happened millions of years ago, Devapriya has to travel back in time. And she does that not with a time machine but with fossils! Fossils are a natural record of living things from the past. They may be imprints on rocks or the actual remains of an ancient plant or animal that has somehow stood the test of time. Devapriya collects the fossils of a group of animals called molluscs.

Most creatures in the mollusc group have a hard shell or 'exoskeleton'. Common examples of these include snails and clams. Shells seen on beaches usually belong to molluscs. These shells are so hardy that they stay preserved over millions of years. So fossils of molluscs are found easily.

The first time she went fossil-hunting, Devapriya was on her own. The sheer joy of discovering these ancient objects made her realize that this was what she wanted to do for the rest of her life. Since then, every year, Devapriya and her team travel to the westernmost part of India, called Kutch. Although the area is dry and barren for much of the year today, Kutch was once under the ocean. This explains why it is so rich in ancient marine fossils. For Devapriya, this makes it the ideal place for her to conduct field studies.

However, there's more to fossil-hunting than merely collecting seashells. Devapriya has to first look at special maps of Kutch that geologists have created over the years. These maps tell her where ancient rocks of different ages are located. She then follows the map to where rocks from the Miocene Era are found. After reaching these sites, she spends the next two weeks crouched over rocks, chiselling and hammering, along with the rest of her team. On some days, it is very hot and extremely tiring, but the effort is well worth it in the end. They return home fifteen to twenty kilos richer in fossils.

Back in her laboratory in Kolkata, Devapriya begins more detailed investigations of her collection. Once she has arranged the fossils from oldest to youngest, she can deduce how a community of molluscs in the area evolved over that period of time. Did they get larger in size or smaller? How did the population of each mollusc species change over time?

She also has a really cool aquarium facility where she keeps real, live mollusc creatures like snails and clams. Devapriya can control the environment in the aquarium. She tweaks the temperature of the water and the chemicals present in it to mimic the past environment and observe how these marine species react to the changes. She then compares their behaviour to that of their ancestors.

Devapriya waits for the day when India will have a research museum that will collect and preserve all the fossils that scientists like her have found. Such a space would allow scientists to share collections and work together to make scientific discoveries faster. People can visit the museum, look at these ancient fossils and understand what they tell us about the history of the earth. Very recently, her crusade for such a museum bore fruit. The government announced that India's first Earth Museum would open to the public soon! It looks like the dream of Devapriya and her palaeontologist friends will finally come true!

INDUMATHI D.

Particle physicist

As a particle physicist, Indu studies some of the smallest particles in the universe—neutrinos. To trap and study these elusive particles, she is planning to build a giant underground observatory!

CATCHING AN INVISIBLE PARTICLE

Indu grew up in Chennai, Tamil Nadu. She still lives there today, spending her days trying to solve the great mysteries of the universe. Her father was a mechanical engineer both at work and at home. So, as a young girl, Indu would often look over his shoulder as he fixed their car, a broken pipe or a malfunctioning radio. Tools scattered on the dining table would delight her to no end and she developed a knack for fixing small things herself.

Indu's first love, however, was cricket. She played for her school team and then was a member of her university team as well. But she hurt a vein in her left ankle while playing in a match in college. The injury was so serious that the doctor worried she might never be able to walk again! Indu happily proved him wrong, but she had to give up cricket. Instead of sulking, though, she turned to her second passion—physics. *What did* matter *really mean*, she wondered. What are the fundamental particles that make up everything we see around us? How do they all work together to make up the universe we see today? She was excited by these questions and eventually chose to become a particle physicist.

As a particle physicist, Indu began to study one of the smallest particles in the universe. But what is the smallest thing in the universe? An atom? No, an atom has a nucleus at its centre. This nucleus is made up of even tinier particles called protons and neutrons. Each proton and neutron is made up of even tinier quarks and gluons.

So then, are quarks and gluons the smallest things in the universe?

Nobody can say for sure. Hundreds of years ago, atoms were thought to be the smallest particles in the universe. But since then, scientists like Indu invented tools such as particle detectors, accelerators and colliders that can study them in great detail. Thanks to these tools, they have discovered a whole set of elementary particles, which are the smallest particles we know about today.

Quarks and gluons are two such elementary particles that combine to form protons and neutrons. These, along with electrons, make up atoms. Atoms constitute most of the matter that we know about—from trees and stones to animals and birds. But Indu was amazed to learn that there is a whole set of particles that exist but are not part of atoms at all. One such elementary particle is the neutrino, Indu's absolute favourite! Neutrinos are everywhere. They whiz across the universe—from the sun and from elsewhere in outer space. Many of them reach us here on earth too. So, how common are they?

Tell you what. Snap your fingers right now. Done? In the amount of time it took you to do this, billions of neutrinos have passed through your thumb! Neutrinos may be tiny, but they are very important because our universe is full of them. Knowing the mass of a neutrino will help Indu understand the rate at which the universe is expanding.

Neutrinos have some very special properties. There are three kinds—the electron neutrino, the muon neutrino, and the tau neutrino. Do you know what the most interesting bit is? Somehow, a single neutrino can morph into different types! That's why Indu wants to spot neutrinos and study them. But the trouble is, neutrinos are really, really small and they carry no electrical charge. This makes them almost impossible to catch.

The only way to catch a travelling neutrino is to wait for it to collide with an atom. When a neutrino collides with an atom, a particle with a tiny electrical charge is released. Think of it as a very tiny spark. If Indu sees a spark, she can tell that there was a neutrino there. That means neutrino hunters like Indu LOVE collisions.

The bad news? Neutrinos almost never collide—with anything! They pass through anything in their way without any sort of interaction. Indu likes to point out that if we lined up seven planets the size of the earth, one after another, a neutrino could go right through all of them without interacting with another particle even once!

But particle physicists never give up. Indu and her friends have a plan. They are planning to build a giant underground observatory under a hill in Tamil Nadu. This is where they will try and catch some neutrinos. Once built, the India-based Neutrino Observatory, or INO, will be the country's most advanced particle physics experiment yet.

The laboratory will house a neutrino detector made out of sheets of iron with detectors sandwiched between them. It will weigh 50,000 tonnes—that is 50,000,000 kg!

This neutrino trap that Indu is helping design will be placed deep underground, almost one kilometre under a hill. This is to filter out the other types of particles that cannot travel through so much rock. When a neutrino collides with an iron atom, the spark created will be detected and Indu and her students will celebrate in the underground lab.

KULJEET
KAUR MARHAS

Planetary scientist

The elements of the universe are chemically evolving. And large exploding stars tell the story of this galactic metallic evolution. Kuljeet, a planetary scientist, is piecing together the story of this cosmic saga with the help of meteorites.

EXPERIMENTS WITH STARDUST

Sardar Singh Marhas had three daughters. His relatives expected every daughter in the family to be *sohni-sohni*—the Punjabi expression for beautiful and pleasant homemakers. Sardar Singh knew his daughters were so much more than that. He had declared proudly: 'My daughters are not meant for the kitchen.'

Kuljeet, one of his daughters, watched her father carefully when he talked about his children. Her father's trust in her made her trust herself. She saw herself through his eyes. She knew she could do and be anything she wanted to be. 'I am a feminist, because my father is one,' says Kuljeet, who took inspiration from her father's love for science. In school, when scrapbooks were passed around, Kuljeet's answer to the question 'What would you like to be in the future?' was always the same—'A scientist'.

And she truly made it happen. Today she is a physicist researching the solar system. She has written several scientific papers about the birth of the sun. Her special interest is in studying tiny pieces of stardust that have been floating in space from the time before the sun was born. The term 'startdust' is used to describe the small bits extracted from meteorites. Can you imagine touching stardust? Kuljeet is the only person in India to have touched this stardust. Not with her bare hands of course, because that would be too risky. What if it falls down and breaks? They are too precious to lose. Locked inside these presolar grains are secrets of not only our sister planets and the sun, but also of the galaxies.

Kuljeet handles stardust with the help of a very special scientific instrument, which is almost as big as an autorickshaw. She has in her lab an amazing machine called NanoSIMS. Her NanoSIMS has around 250 knobs and adjustments! It is hard work to use this machine but once you learn how to do it, it can tell you the secrets of the stars.

Kuljeet wonders how our beautiful solar system was born. Where did it all come from? With her amazing machine, she can find clues about what happened before the sun, the moon and all the planets all came to be.

From time to time, space agencies send robots to space to bring back samples from asteroids and comets. Very few scientists in the world receive these samples. Kuljeet is the only one in India working on pieces of the comet Itokawa, which were collected by the Japanese space agency JAXA.

She also studies grains from meteorites that fall on to the earth from space. Doing astronomy without sending telescopes and robots into space is jokingly called the 'poor man's space programme'. 'Because stardust comes to your house, you don't have to go anywhere. It falls down right in front of you and you are lucky if it is very, very old,' Kuljeet says.

Besides revealing the secrets of our solar system, Kuljeet's samples from space tell us about the origin of metals like iron, chromium, nickel and some other elements. All these elements are formed during the lifetimes of stars. When a really big star dies, it explodes in a big beautiful spectacle called a supernova. During a supernova, heavy metals made by the star are expelled into space from its core. And when gravity collects all this expelled matter and brings it together, new stars and their star systems are born.

The quantity of elements in the universe that are heavier than the lightest of the elements—hydrogen and helium (the basic star stuff with minimal neutrons, protons and electrons)—increases with the dying of each star. When stars die, with time, they make the universe richer in metals. 'The galaxy is evolving in its metallicity, we call this galactic chemical evolution,' Kuljeet says.

This is the area of research that Kuljeet enjoys the most. Her powerful NanoSIMS machine can find out what the tiny bits from space are made of, along with how they came to be. Often, the pieces she does her experiments on are even older than the sun. NanoSIMS helps her determine the true age of the elements that make up the piece she is studying.

However, when the machine first arrived at her lab in Ahmedabad, Kuljeet was in for a shock. Just as it arrived from France, this expensive machine, which cost 14 crore rupees, fell down and broke!

The broken NanoSIMS was shipped back to the manufacturers. Fixing it took an entire year. When it came back, it still wasn't in working condition. Now it was up to Kuljeet to fix the only NanoSIMS in India. She did this all alone as she had no staff in her lab. This was a really tough time for Kuljeet. She fixed the machine herself even as she was expecting a child. She continued working on the machine until her daughter was a few months old.

The hard work paid off. Today, Kuljeet happily uses the machine to research stardust to reveal the secrets of our solar system

HANSIKA
KAPOOR
Psychologist

Hansika is an experimental cognitive psychologist, who is happy to attach wires to your head to find out the whys and hows of cheating in exams, playing pranks and all the other not-so-wise ideas our brains come up with.

FOR THE SAKE OF SCIENCE

Hansika Kapoor believes in doing science for the sake of science. Her scientific work is not aimed at new inventions but at simply finding answers. Hers is not a quest to discover a miracle drug or to invent some game-changing technology. Her goal is to use the power of science to find out why humans behave the way they do.

In school, Hansika's textbooks were filled with caricatures of her teachers. Her doodles made her realize that boredom pushes people into being creative. As a teenager, Hansika had an avid interest in the lives of painters and artists. She was obsessed with knowing what went through the minds of creative geniuses when they were creating art. Van Gogh, a European painter who led life in poverty and despair, was Hansika's favourite artist. *Did his angst make him creative?* Hansika wondered.

Van Gogh is still Hansika's favourite artist. And now, as a grown-up, she is a cognitive and social psychologist who still studies creativity. Why do people swear? What role do our emotions play when we make daily decisions about things like taking a bath, brushing our teeth or going to school? Do we like to gossip about people who are different from us? Why do we admire our favourite superheroes and why do we sometimes want to be superheroes ourselves? What makes our brains creative? These are some of the questions that Hansika has tried to answer in her psychology experiments.

Hansika knows that the brain and its ability to learn are related to how we behave. Besides the biology of our brains, social conditions around us dictate our behaviour as well. This seems obvious, but just an intuitive feeling is not good enough for Hansika, who puts her trust only in science. 'Science doesn't work like that. There needs to be evidence and data to actually show why people behave a certain way,' she believes.

So Hansika performs experiments. In fact, she performs many experiments to get a very large set of results. Only then can she be sure that the conclusions she is making are as accurate as possible. One of her recent big projects researched *negative* creativity. 'Negative creativity is when one uses creativity for a goal that is not considered "good",' Hansika explains. One example is finding a new way to cheat in an exam.

Hansika set out to find if there was a difference between brain activity when creativity was used for good versus when creativity was used for bad.

In her experiments, she asked over 600 participants to come up with both positive and negative creative behaviours. Thirty-six of them were strapped to EEG—electroencephalogram—machines. The EEG measures brain activity by recording the rising and falling levels of a frequency called alpha power in our brains. In average humans, this frequency ranges between 8 hertz and 12 hertz. Researchers have found that alpha power is fired in the brain when human beings are being creative. Hansika used this tried-and-tested fact as the basis for her own research.

Building on other people's existing research is how science goes forward. Hansika loves this about science. She is happy to add her own little contribution to the big pool of existing psychology research. With each paper she writes, science moves forward. 'I don't think a research paper of mine will change the world. But it is one step closer to something that might,' she says.

Hansika loves writing research papers. She has published many and helped other people write their own. With her friends and her brother, she has started a small research institute in Mumbai where they do amazing research about our society and its psychology, while also training budding scientists in research methodology and the use of statistics.

At this research institute, Hansika leads the psychology department, where a lot of interesting and critical psychological research takes place. Since Hansika has never been abroad, she calls herself a 'homegrown researcher'. She feels social science research is not taught well in India and that most people don't even understand what social scientists do. These are things she is determined to change.

BHARATI
INDIAN RESEARCH BASE
LAT 69°24.271'S
LONG 76°12.147'E

MANGALA
MANI
Satellite engineer

Mangala is an expert in processing the signals that come from satellites in space. In this pursuit, she once spent 403 days on the barren, freezing continent of Antarctica!

Fourteen Frozen Months

For 403 days, all Mangala Mani saw was vast swathes of white. As much as the fifty-six-year-old engineer would have loved to sit and stare at the stark beauty of the Antarctic landscapes, she had a job to finish. Bundled up in layers of warm clothing, she and two more engineers from India's space agency ISRO would bravely step out to face the freezing winds and barren land on which the Bharati Research Station was situated.

Bharati is India's third Antarctic research facility. This is where the three engineers spent their days and nights tirelessly converting satellite data into a form that is readable by her colleagues back at the National Remote Sensing Centre in Hyderabad. They were part of a twenty-three-member team who occupied the research station from late 2016 to December 2017.

Growing up in Hyderabad, Mangala had always been fascinated by geography and problem-solving. Ever since she read a newspaper article about Mars, she began harbouring dreams of working for a space agency. Noticing their daughter's keen interest, Mangala's parents helped her enrol in a technical course at a nearby college. After studying in an all-girls' high school, Mangala now found herself the only girl in a class of eighty students. During this course, she had the opportunity to spend time in some of the biggest factories and plants in India. For Mangala, these were small but crucial steps towards her ultimate dream—to join India's space agency ISRO.

She was ecstatic when she received an appointment letter to join ISRO right out of college, but there was still one big hurdle. Her parents thought it was not safe to send her away from home. This was frustrating for her because Mangala always believed that there was nothing that girls can't do. All that a person needs to fulfil their dream is a little bit of courage and Mangala had plenty. Thanks to a supportive uncle, she was able to convince her parents to let her go.

Today, Mangala works at ISRO's National Remote Sensing Centre in Hyderabad. She is an expert in processing the signals that come from remote sensing satellites in space. These are one of the most useful classes of satellites because they contain cameras that collect information about the earth's resources from afar, or 'remotely'.

Why go all the way to space to take pictures of the earth? Because space gives us the best view, of course. Earlier, space agencies used to send aircraft with cameras to perform remote sensing but this is too expensive a practice. Satellites, once launched, can orbit around the earth for years and they take less blurry pictures. They can be controlled from ground stations like Bharati in Antarctica and this is the job of technical scientists like Mangala.

The advantage of having a research station in Antarctica is that its skies are ideal for satellite tracking. The more research stations there are on the ground, the better equipped ISRO is to handle the vast amounts of data that is received. Mangala and the other engineers at ISRO use equipment and computer programmes to tell the satellite where it should be looking and also to monitor its health and fix any problems. Most importantly, Mangala is involved in processing the signals received from the satellites.

The signals from remote sensing satellites look like gibberish at first. Mangala converts them into a language that our computers can interpret in order to give us useful information regarding monitoring crops and rainfall, as well as managing natural disasters. When flash floods struck north India, Mangala and her team provided crucial inputs that helped rescue teams carry out their life-saving missions.

ISRO has launched several remote sensing satellites over the years and around eleven of them are actively orbiting the earth today. These satellites function 24/7, so Mangala's work never stops. Nevertheless, the members of her team work in shifts so that they each have time to rest and play sports for exercise.

Mangala is the first woman scientist to be part of an ISRO wintering team at Antarctica. 'Wintering' projects go on for over a year and include the worst of the winter—May, June and July—when there is no sunlight. The temperature during these months dips down to minus 40 degrees Celsius! During winter (from March to November), even the few animals that live here such as penguins, seals, skuas, snow petrels and storm petrels disappear into hibernation. Mangala only had her fellow team-members for company.

Before going on such an extreme mission, Mangala needed to strengthen not just her body but also her mind. Her family, especially her children, gave her all the motivation she needed. She also prepared for the harsh environment by trekking up the Himalayas with her colleagues to build strength and team spirit. After a series of safety and security training sessions as well as many medical check-ups, she was ready to undertake the scientific trip to Antarctica.

None of this felt too dangerous or impossible to Mangala. She was determined to contribute to science. For a scientist, what better way to do this than with an adventure in an isolated and mysterious land like Antarctica! Despite having accomplished so much, Mangala has not forgotten her childhood dream of earning a PhD. If braving the Antarctic is possible at the age of fifty-six, then she knows nothing can stop her.

SOUMYA PRASAD

Forest ecologist

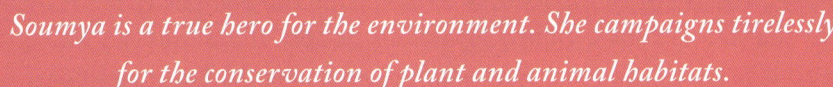

Soumya is a true hero for the environment. She campaigns tirelessly for the conservation of plant and animal habitats.

DISPERSING THE SEEDS OF SCIENCE

Soumya grew up in Bengaluru, a city that is home to a lot of scientific institutions. As a little girl, she went to the planetarium often and enjoyed visiting science laboratories in the city when they opened their doors to the public. These experiences inspired her to become a scientist herself.

Her summer vacations were spent in different forests of India as she accompanied her wildlife photographer father and nature-loving mother. The young Soumya developed a passion for animals, trees, rivers and streams. These experiences paved the way for her lifelong focus on the happenings in Indian forests.

After graduating in wildlife conservation from a college in north India, Soumya studied the forest trees in the Western Ghats for many years. She then took some time off in the rainforests of the Anaimalai Hills in Tamil Nadu. During her free time there, she wandered the area to take down details of all the woody plants in the forest. As a natural historian, she had become very aware of the threats to trees from human-induced climate change. She wanted to be sure that all the species of trees in this forest were accounted for before they were lost to climate change.

Climate change is bringing unforeseen changes in the habitats that people, animals and plants live in. As we see today, the number of extreme climate events like floods, heatwaves and droughts is on the rise. It is expected that climate change will cause several million people to migrate to other places on the planet as their homes become unliveable.

People can get on an airplane or take a train to move to new homes, but how do plants move to newer environments? 'Plants rely on seeds for migration,' Soumya says. The seeds of plants take a ride inside the animals that eat their fruits. Wherever the animal goes, until the animal poops, the seeds go along. This is called seed dispersal—the natural phenomenon closest to Soumya's heart.

Much of Soumya's research involves observing how animals and trees interact inside forests. Sometimes, she tags animals with transmitters to track their movement. On most field study days, her eyes stay fixed on fruit trees because animals love to eat pulpy fruits. She observes and records everything that happens.

One summer day, at the Rajaji Nature Reserve in Uttarakhand, she made an amazing discovery. She was there to identify the animals that eat a fruit called amla (the Indian gooseberry). Some scientists believed it to be the hornbill bird but Soumya found that it wasn't. The animals she observed eating amla and dispersing its seeds were deer—chital and barking deer. But deer couldn't reach the fruits on the amla tree on their own, so how were they doing it? She was awestruck to witness the ecosystem helping them out. There was another animal partnering with the deer to help disperse amla.

One day, in the forest, Soumya saw that deer follow langurs in the forest during the six-month-long amla fruiting season. Langurs jump from one tree to another to eat amla. They eat some of the pulp and drop the rest of the fruit to the ground. Deer waiting below then eat the dropped fruits. 'Also, langurs are very clumsy—when they move, they bring down all the fruit,' Soumya says.

'Deer? They are seed destroyers, they don't help trees disperse their seeds,' some scientists said when Soumya published her findings. But Soumya proved them wrong by making another important discovery. She saw that the deer were in fact dispersing amla seeds by vomiting the seeds. The scientists who claimed deer were seed destroyers had only checked their stomachs and poop to see if they contained the seeds of the fruit they had eaten. When they didn't find any, they thought that the deer ground the seeds with their teeth and destroyed them. Soumya went a step further and checked their vomit too. That was when she realized that amla seeds were too big to pass through the second chamber of the deer stomachs. She proved that deer were in fact very helpful seed dispersers.

Everyone needs to hear about such scientific facts that ecologists like Soumya are finding out. If they don't, they might take the ecosystem for granted and fail to protect it. 'There is a lot of science about nature conservation that is just piling up, there is also the plastic ban but it does not have much impact in the real world. I feel this is a communication problem,' Soumya says.

With better communication and collaboration between communities, we can take steps together to protect the biodiversity of our forests. To spread the message of nature conservation and to share the knowledge that scientists like her are gathering, Soumya has started a non-governmental organization or an NGO not far from Rajaji National Park, where she made her discoveries. Here, Soumya continues her research and is working on building a sustainability centre to show that, with science-based solutions, it is possible to live a modern life without harming nature.

KUSALA RAJENDRAN

Seismologist

Earthquakes are a tremendous mystery. Kusala does the detective work with the help of long lost poems and pottery shards under the sea.

SNIFFING FOR EARTHQUAKES

As a young girl, Kusala's ambition was to be a teacher. She liked all her teachers at school and aspired to be like them. While she was pursuing her master's degree, her professors ignited her curiosity to study the earth. 'I have become a teacher and a scientist, just like I wished. I love what I am doing,' she says.

Science is interrelated. The topics that scientists are researching today can be really complex. They no longer fall under a single umbrella like physics, geology or meteorology. To keep things simple, Kusala calls herself an 'earth scientist'. But, specifically, Kusala studies earthquakes.

Among the many mysteries of the earth, Kusala teaches her students why we are unable to predict earthquakes. Unlike most other natural disasters, earthquakes are quite hard to predict. Even for other natural phenomena that can be seen, felt and tracked—such as rain—making an accurate prediction is impossible. It's even worse with earthquakes. 'With earthquakes, nothing is observable!' Kusala says.

Kusala uses evidence from recent earthquakes to develop the history of earthquakes in an area. It is a bit like solving a puzzle. She comes up with the best guess about the approximate location and size of past earthquakes by piecing together clues from recent earthquakes. In the absence of other evidence, this data is useful because they can help to tell if an earthquake will happen again. Such information is useful when planning developmental activities in these areas such as setting up of a nuclear power plant or constructing a large reservoir of water.

Being in the field of earthquake prediction can be risky business, as some earth scientists in Italy will agree. In 2008, six of them were convicted of murder because they reassured the people of L'Aquila that a major earthquake would not follow the small tremors that the town had been experiencing. But a powerful earthquake did follow and many people died.

Kusala has herself also issued reassurances about earthquakes on the radio, but only when she is reasonably sure. 'This was for a region in Kerala where even moderate earthquakes have not occurred during documented history. Moreover, recent tectonic history does not warrant destructive earthquakes in the region.' she said. Even though she stands behind her science, she makes it a point to add: 'With anything in nature there is always an element of the unknown.'

Earthquakes are a result of movement of large plates that form the outer, approximately 100-km-thick shell of the earth. When these tectonic plates rub against each other, the earth shakes. With it, all of our buildings, roads, water bodies and we, ourselves are shaken. The regions of friction between the plates are defined by weak zones, known as faults. For example, the Himalayas define an active fault zone. These mountains were formed when the plates of India and Eurasia collided. It is a region that experiences many earthquakes. If the earthquake is strong, there is a great risk of loss of lives and infrastructure close to the epicentre of the earthquake. When an earthquake takes place on the ocean floor, it might give rise to massive waves or a tsunami that can flood large areas, destroying them completely. Keeping a watch on fault lines and seismic activity is very important. And scientists like Kusala are here to do that.

She and her husband are an earthquake-tracking team; they have worked together for many years and have authored more than forty papers together. One seismic mystery they solved took place in the coastal town of Kaveripattinam in Tamil Nadu. The town had been ravaged by the 2004 Indian Ocean earthquake and tsunami—an event that was considered quite unusual, even by experts. Kusala and her husband wanted to find out if an earthquake had taken place before in the same area. They found a clue in an ancient Tamil poem called *Manimekhalai* that narrates the story of the sea swallowing up the town because the ruling Chola King angered the gods by missing an annual religious festival. Religious reasons aside, did this really happen? And could this have been a tsunami? The hunch that Kusala and her husband had was proven to be right. In their investigations of the area, they found 1000-year-old pottery shards and other evidence that proved that there had indeed been a tsunami in the area.

Kusala feels India's potential as an earth science hub is not fully explored. For example, the Himalayas are the most active plate-collision boundary in the world, and there is so much work to be done here. There is a lot more to discover about the past of the earth that will help us make it a better and safer place to live on.

NAMRATA GUPTA

Sociologist

When women in science are so awesome, why are they not as famous as their male counterparts? And why are they rarer to find in Indian universities and institutes? Sociologist Namrata questions Indian scientists of all genders to find the answers.

BRIDGING THE GENDER GAP IN SCIENCE

Namrata found her way into science through history. She loved books on history, especially the histories of strong women. When she was old enough, she wrote her master's thesis on the position of women in society through history. Subjects like the history of society and science might seem like they are worlds apart, but there are many connections between them. 'Science is in fact a social process because it cannot be done alone. It requires interaction among many people, laboratories and organizations,' Namrata says.

For her PhD, Namrata combined the sociology of science—the study of the lives of people involved in science—with her interest in the progress of women. A statistic she came across shocked her so much that she quickly framed her research question around this: why are there so few women in science?

The statistic she saw in 1999 reported that 36 per cent of people training in science in India were women. Yet, only 10 per cent of Indian scientists were women. Scientific institutes in the country had almost no women bosses. These statistics remain almost unchanged today. And many years after her PhD, Namrata continues to look for the answers behind this gender gap.

No matter what you feel like—a boy, a girl, neither or somewhere in between—it should not dictate what you do in your life. There are a lot more similarities than differences among people of different genders, don't you think? No geneticist, psychologist or neurologist has ever found that men are better at doing science than women. In fact, all the amazing women scientists through history, although fewer in number than their famous male counterparts, proves that women are really good at science. Then why are the numbers so different?

The answer to this question, according to Namrata, lies in the sociology of science. It is true that fewer women are doing science, but this is not because they can't or don't want to. Namrata has been researching the gender gap in Indian science for twenty years. She uses two of a sociologist's favoured methods—in-depth interviews and surveys. To get to the bottom of the gender gap in science, she has examined the work life of 500 men and women engaged in scientific research in the country.

One of her main findings is the proverbial 'glass ceiling' that prevents women from moving ahead in science. This is an invisible barrier between women and top positions in science. The reasons behind the existence of the barrier are many. There are no actual rules that discriminate against women. Discrimination

stems from the ways in which the existing rules are applied. For instance, Namrata found that teams that hired scientists questioned women's commitment towards the job because of their gender. She also found that the scientific work women do is often underestimated by everyone.

In many institutes in India, couples are not allowed to work within the same institute. This rule often prevents wives from working in the same towns as their husbands and vice versa. Many women end up sacrificing their preferences, and they are sometimes forced to give up scientific research altogether. Many women that Namrata interviewed told her that they could not find as much time for science as they wanted to because the institutions they worked at did not have day care centres for their children.

'Since for a long time, scientific institutes have been composed mainly of men, the life at these institutes is based on the dominance of men,' Namrata says. Many people in our country assume women lack devotion to science because their focus is on taking care of their families and children. One result of these assumptions is that office policies like paid family leave or maternity leave is offered only to mothers and not fathers. This reinforces the stereotype that childcare is the duty of the mother alone. Thus, even the informal environment at the workplace like hearing women out at meetings show the gender biases that exist in society.

Science is collaborative. Working with other experts takes science forward. Namrata's research has found that women scientists tend to be excluded from the scientific community and do not make as many professional contacts as men do. They are neither invited to as many scientific meetings nor are they nominated for awards by their male colleagues. 'Women lose out in a major way because they depend heavily only on their hard work and merit (that is, human capital). They do not have the full benefit of the professional network that their male colleagues enjoy because they are not welcomed into networks as easily as men are. Women in science have confessed to Namrata that they have to work twice as hard as men. This is not fair.

As Indian science moves forward and becomes more conscious of its gender bias, Namrata plans to continue her research on women in science. She is highlighting the changes taking place in our scientific institutions as more and more women scientists are seen reflecting critically on the current policies.

'Social scientists are needed to make good policies for the people of the country. Without knowing how society works, how can you bring about any change?' she says.

NANDITA
SRIVASTAVA
Astrophysicist

An observatory in the middle of a lake in Rajasthan is a great place to observe the sun. Nandita started her research journey here as a student and today is in charge of a unique solar observatory that keeps a watch on our fiery sun.

THE TELESCOPE ISLAND

Nandita grew up in a family of scholars. Her dad is a physicist and her mother is a history professor. When she started college, her older sister went off to do research in physics, leaving Nandita behind with articles and books written by the famous Indian astronomer Jayant Narlikar. When it was time for Nandita to choose a subject to study, she chose astrophysics. She wanted to be a scientist. 'There was never any other goal in my mind,' she says.

In her college, close to home in Madhya Pradesh, she proved to be a bright student and was selected to attend the national workshop on solar physics. But going there involved a three-day journey to Kodaikanal in the south of India by changing three trains. 'At the time, I was too timid to travel alone this far,' Nandita says. Thankfully, her professor offered to accompany her and encouraged her to attend the workshop.

The one-week workshop initiated Nandita into solar physics. She was surrounded by top scientists discussing unanswered questions in solar physics. This motivated and inspired her to take up solar physics research. Today, Nandita heads the Udaipur Solar Observatory in Rajasthan and has won awards for her work on solar eruptions.

Just as a weather forecaster predicts if the following week will be cloudy, windy or rainy, Nandita, a solar astronomer, predicts weather in space. Weather conditions in the solar system are dictated by the sun's activity. So, as a space weather forecaster, Nandita has her eyes fixed on the sun all the time. Of course, this would be a painful thing to do with the naked eye and doesn't tell you anything about the eruptions on the surface of the sun.

The sun is a middle-aged star in the prime of its life. It repeatedly goes through eleven-year cycles. During five-and-a-half years of the cycle, the sun is intensely active with many eruptions on its surface, spewing plasma, radiation and magnetic storms in the interplanetary space. The other half of the cycle is the calmer phase.

Depending on its speed, it takes between one to four days for a solar storm to reach the earth. It is crucial that we know when and how these solar storms travel towards us as they could potentially harm technology that humans depend on like electric grids.

For almost eighteen years, Nandita has been on a mission to find out when, why and how eruptions on the surface of the sun take place. To do this, she requires observations of the sun made by ground-based and space-based telescopes. Analysing the pictures of the sun taken by telescopes helps her identify solar features that lead to radiation storms in our interplanetary space.

Although scientists have been continuously observing the sun for two entire solar cycles—that is, for twenty-two years—there is not enough data to fully understand the origins of solar eruptions. Using telescopes and observatories, solar astronomers all over the world are putting their brains together to solve the puzzle. Nandita is one of them. She often travels to solar astronomy centres all over the world to look at their collected data and discuss her own results with the teams there. 'Scientists cannot work in isolation, it is almost impossible. You have to take data from multiple telescopes and instruments to make your interpretations more accurate,' she says.

Nandita's favourite sun-viewing spot is the Udaipur Solar Observatory (USO) in Rajasthan. This houses the most sophisticated solar telescope in India, at this time. USO is very special since the telescope is located in the middle of a lake. Such an arrangement, where the telescope is surrounded by water rather than solid ground, is an innovative way to avoid the 'ground-heating' effect that can make the pictures from ground-based telescopes very blurry. Another reason that makes the telescope so great is the fact that Rajasthan receives very little rainfall and the sun shines bright most of the year, making it an ideal location for a solar observatory.

Nandita joined USO as a PhD student and every day for the four years during her research, she took a boat to the telescope in the middle of the lake, observed the sun through it all day and returned at sunset to analyse the data she collected. After being awarded a PhD, she went abroad for postdoctoral work before returning to USO. She now leads the group at USO where the old telescope from her PhD days has been replaced with a new and improved one—the Multi-Application Solar Telescope or MAST.

The MAST telescope at USO looks at the lower layers of the sun—the photospheric layers and the chromospheric layers—where solar eruptions originate. It can detect sunspots—the dark dots on the sun's surface that indicate intense activity—in good detail and also records the magnetic field measurements on the sun's surface. If there is a big change in magnetic field parameters, Nandita expects a big eruption. Being a top scientist in the field, Nandita is opening doors for India's future solar missions. With other Indian astronomers, she is building ADITYA, the Indian spaceship that will travel towards the sun in 2020.

JYOTSNA DHAWAN

Stem cell biologist

How do muscle stem cells decide whether to stay quiet or to become active? If they decide to stay quiet, how do they know when they need to wake up? Jyotsna is on a mission to identify how cells control this behaviour.

THE SILENCE OF THE CELLS

Jyotsna Dhawan grew up in the city of Bengaluru surrounded by scientists. Her father studied aeroplanes and rockets, and her mother was a botanist. Inspired by the scientific chatter around the dinner table, her brother would grow up to become an astronomer and her sister would be an artist who works with clay—which, in case you think isn't about science, actually involves lots of chemistry! And Jyotsna was not going to be left behind. She too had grown to love the beauty of nature and art and soon, she began to see the beauty of science.

While studying biology in college, Jyotsna spent a lot of her time exploring nature. She loved the time she spent among wild trees and flowers in leech-filled rainforests, so much so that she was sure she would spend her life doing that. However one day, she happened to look through a powerful microscope and her mind was blown! The idea that it was possible to grow individual cells in a laboratory and have them divide while you watched them was a revelation to her. She was especially drawn to muscle cells because you could see them twitch in the dish. She learned that cell biologists hoped to one day develop a cure for many life-threatening muscular disorders that affect people all over the world. She decided to join them. Today, she works in a laboratory in Hyderabad solving mysteries of skeletal muscles.

Skeletal muscles are the muscles attached to our bones. They allow us to move around and account for almost half of our body weight. If you ask Jyotsna to flex her muscles, she might not show you her biceps. Instead, she might give you a wide smile. She calls the muscle a very 'human' tissue because they allow us to smile or frown or raise our eyebrows in surprise when we hear that there are forty-three different muscles in the face!

Every human being starts off as a single cell inside their mother's body. That cell keeps multiplying to form a ball of identical cells. When the ball is big enough, it becomes a busy place. The cells have to divide tasks among themselves to keep growing. Some become blood cells, others skin cells, lung cells and so on. But some cells don't get any tasks. They just wait silently. They don't multiply, but they don't get assigned a job either. These silent cells are called stem cells. Are they completely useless? No, they're just the opposite! They save lives by acting as substitutes. Whenever a specific tissue type gets damaged, these stem cells wake up and take the place of the damaged tissue. The stem cells lie within muscles, sleeping on top of the muscle fibres, between two thin sheets of protein. They are alive but quiet, ever ready to play the role of muscle cells whenever needed.

106

How do cells decide whether to stay quiet as a stem cell or to become an active muscle cell? If they decide to stay quiet, how do they know when they need to wake up? Something must be controlling these things, Jyotsna guessed. Some sort of a 'switch', perhaps?

To spot this switch, Jyotsna and her team peer through microscopes, observing how stem cells behave. They also grow millions of cells in a special dish and then break them apart in a test tube to sift through the proteins inside them. After years of chasing different proteins, Jyotsna's student Sirisha found something interesting about a protein called PRDM2. It looked like stem cells needed PRDM2 to remain quiet. When a cell doesn't have PRDM2, it is active. Excited, Jyotsna advised Sirisha to do more rounds of testing, this time helped by two more of her students, Deepika and Amena. Together, Jyotsna and the three young women pieced together the puzzle: PRDM2 acts as a 'PAUSE' button, directing cells to stay silent. Eureka! Jyotsna's team had found their switch!

There's no time to rest, however. Experiments all over the world show that there are many more switches working together to make sure that these sleeping stem cells wake up when they need to. If not, our muscles would be in trouble! If stem cells do not wake up on command, then they will not be able to rush in and replace damaged muscle cells; on the other hand, if they wake up out of turn, the cells will keep growing into a lump of useless tissue that doesn't twitch like muscle should.

Solving these biological mysteries is critical for people who have muscle disorders. Such disorders are most common among the elderly, but they also occur in people who are born with them or have been injured seriously. Take muscular dystrophy, for example. A person with muscular dystrophy has very weak muscles because the muscle cells die at a faster rate than they should. For a while, their muscle stem cells will jump to the task of replacing these lost cells, but over time, the number of stem cells dwindles and the number required is much greater than the number produced. Similarly, when we grow old, the body begins to run out of healthy stem cells. Even if the stem cells are present, if their switches don't work correctly, they cannot perform their duties on time. The more information Jyotsna and others gather about these switches, the more likely it is that incurable diseases like muscular dystrophy can finally be treated.

The most exciting moments in science for Jyotsna are not the ones that make her say 'Eureka!', but the ones that make her go 'Hmm, that's strange'. So, the next time you think *hmm, that's strange*, start investigating! You never know—it could be the beginning of a great discovery!

SHIKHA VARMA

Condensed matter physicist

Shikha specializes in surface science. This means that her job is to study the outermost layer of many materials. Thanks to hi-tech gadgets, Shikha can zoom into a single layer of atoms on the surface of her sample.

Surface Science for a Solar Future

Shikha Varma is from Fatehgarh, a town in Uttar Pradesh. Although she enjoyed science classes in school, her most memorable times were spent with her brother and father working on small home projects. The three would scour newspapers and magazines to make scrapbooks and collages of exciting scientific developments. Newspaper cuttings of historic events like the moon landing in 1969 were all stored safely.

By the time she finished school, Shikha decided she hadn't had enough of her favourite subject, physics. So, she chose to continue studying it in college. Watching her professors at work, she realized that it was possible to explore the whys and hows of the universe for a living. So Shikha decided to pursue a career in physics. She trained in different laboratories in the United States of America before starting her own lab at a university in Bhubaneswar almost twenty-five years ago. For many years, she was the only woman scientist there!

Shikha's laboratory houses different kinds of materials and highly specialized gadgets that can tweak materials, and examine and change their properties.

Did you know that there are over a hundred elements that have been identified so far? All 118 of these are listed in the periodic table. Each of these elements has its own unique qualities. Studying the atoms that make up an element can explain why they behave the way they do. This is why chemists and physicists have spent many years doing this. Knowing the properties of elements allows us to choose the right one for the right purpose. The element aluminium, for example, is light. This is why it is used to make aircrafts and thin foil. Shikha's favourite element, however, is gold, which is a popular choice for making jewellery because of how shiny it is. Gold is also considered inert, meaning it does not rust like iron or react with other elements easily.

But Shikha would disagree with this. Doing research in condensed matter physics proved to her that gold isn't always inert. Very, very tiny grains of gold are, in fact, reactive! So the properties do not vary only from element to element, but also within the same element, especially when its particle size is too small. Scientists' attempts to understand this gave birth to the field of surface science.

Shikha specializes in surface science. This means that her job is to study the outermost layer of materials. How thick is this layer? Picture the tip of a hair on the antenna of a baby ant. Now imagine something a thousand times thinner than that. These levels are called 'nano' scales. A nanometre measures one-millionth of a millimetre. Thanks to hi-tech gadgets, Shikha can zoom into a single layer of atoms on the surface of her sample.

More than gold, however, Shikha is fascinated by the surface properties of another material—titania, which is the common name for titanium dioxide. Usually a white powder, it has been a common ingredient in everyday products like paints, cosmetics and plastics for years now. But it also promises to be something much more. Recently, scientists have uncovered that titania can absorb certain kinds of light, making it potentially useful to store solar energy.

The problem is that titania mostly absorbs ultraviolet light. Since sunlight is predominantly made up of another type of light called visible light (which comprises VIBGYOR, the colours of the rainbow that we can see), the power of titania is limited. Shikha decided that she would try to alter the properties of titania so that it absorbs visible light better.

With a number of trusty and hi-tech gadgets by her side, Shikha started her experiments. She took a small sample of titania and put it inside a special chamber. This chamber had all the air sucked out of it so that the titania was in something called an ultra-high vacuum. Shikha then directed a beam of positively-charged atoms to the titania sample. The ions were made of the element argon. When the positively-charged argon atoms hit the surface of the titania sample, something peculiar happened. Shikha observed, through her powerful atomic force microscope, that the titania surface had been altered. It had become studded with tiny nanostructures. She discovered that these titania nanostructures have special powers. They can absorb much more visible light and hence store much more solar energy than normal titania.

Given the energy crisis the world is facing today, developing sustainable energy options like solar energy is incredibly important. Having a powerful substance like titania absorb more solar energy could be a giant step in this direction. Titania can be used to make sun-powered batteries, that is, solar cells, as well as to clean up oil spills in the ocean by breaking down oil molecules. Thanks to discoveries by Shikha and other physicists, scientists are more confident today about the potential of titania.

29

BHARGAVI SRINIVASULU

Chiropterologist

As a chiropterologist, Bhargavi travels to lots of different places looking for bats. She enjoys getting dirty, crawling into caves and scaling vertical walls. Along the way, she has also managed to discover some lost species!

FOLLOWING FLYING MAMMALS

Growing up in Hyderabad, Bhargavi was fiercely protected by her conservative family. She did not always have a grand ambition for the future, but since she was best at biology, she chose to study it in college. It was after she met Chelmala Srinivasulu, her research partner and now also her husband, that she realized how exciting a life in science could be. Fascinated by his research on fruit-eating bats, Bhargavi realized that bats were crucial to our ecosystem and that there were far too few people studying them. So she began doing her own research on insect-eating bats.

Bhargavi's biggest adventure as a bat scientist or a chiropterologist came in 2013 in a district in Karnataka called Kolar, which is sometimes known as the land of silk, milk and gold. Gold-mining in Kolar ended many years ago, but the district continues to be active in the dairy and silk industries. However, it was none of these that led a determined Bhargavi and her team of chiropterologists there. It was the promise of finding bats.

And not just any bat. The Kolar leaf-nosed bat. Very little was known about this species of bat other than the fact that they were discovered by some scientists in 1974. These scientists did not identify them correctly at first. They left no specific notes except the fact that the bats lived in some caves in a village there. Only in 1994 did scientists realize that these bats belonged to a new species called *Hipposideros hypophyllus*, which is the scientific name of the Kolar leaf-nosed bat.

This species had not been seen since 1994. As a result, it made it to the International Union for Conservation of Nature's 'Red List' of endangered species. But exactly how much danger these bats were in was not really known. Spurred on by the mysterious status of these elusive bats, Bhargavi went to Kolar to find them.

Bhargavi started her quest by first talking to the local people. At first, no one gave a positive response to her questions about the bats. After days of bad luck, she was starting to lose hope when she had a chance encounter with an elderly man. He claimed to know a cave where the bats might be still living. Hoping for the best, Bhargavi followed his directions. She found the cave and crawled inside to investigate. Immediately, she was hit by a very strong smell of bat poop. It was clear that bats lived in this cave, but were they Kolar leaf-nosed bats?

To find out, she had to wait till night-time, when the bats wake up and get busy. With the help of her chiropterologist friends, she put up a net between two poles. As they had hoped, a few bats flew into these nets. Bhargavi peered in closely at the captured bats and cried out in victory. The Kolar leaf-nosed bat had been rediscovered! Bhargavi and her team took the first ever photographs of this species.

They were able to estimate that only about 200 of these bats remain on earth, so there was an urgent need of conservation efforts before they go extinct. The bats are now labelled 'critically endangered', so the local people and government of Kolar now know that they must protect these bats and their habitats.

Often, people ask Bhargavi—'what is the big deal about bats?' She has three replies to this:

1. They drink nectar from night-blooming flowers and help in the pollination of many fruits and vegetables.
2. They eat fruits and spit out seeds. These seeds sprout into plants and trees, helping in forest regeneration.
3. A single bat can eat up to 4,000 mosquitoes a night, making them a natural way to control mosquito populations and mosquito-borne diseases.

Bats can set up their homes in many different kinds of habitats—in forests and even in cities. In her pursuit of them, Bhargavi gets to travel to lots of different places. She enjoys getting dirty, crawling into tiny spaces, and scaling vertical walls. She does not even mind the smell of bat poop! Many superstitions about bats exist in society—for example, some say they are a bad omen, they will fly into your ears, etc. But these are not true. Bhargavi knows that bats are as harmless as most other animals. Unfortunately, these myths lead people to destroy bat homes.

Bhargavi works at a university and lives with her family of bat lovers. Her husband and her son are chiropterologists too. And the three of them are always planning their next batty adventure.

ROHINI
LAKSHANE
Technologist

30

The right to Internet access is a fundamental right of every Indian citizen. Rohini is a technologist and activist upholding this right by studying the instances where it is taken away.

KNOWLEDGE AND TECHNOLOGY FOR ALL

When Rohini was growing up, watching TV was not appreciated in the Lakshane household. Instead of the TV, the Internet and books became the teenage Rohini's sources of entertainment and information. The books her parents encouraged her to read brought her attention to the inequalities and injustices that exist in human society.

Rohini grew up believing that all people are equal. Why do some people have more money and opportunities than others, even though the laws of nature are same for everyone? Rohini pondered over what could be done to make a more equal society.

In college, Rohini understood that the laws of a country have everything to do with how its society functions. Opportunities to live a well-informed, happy and healthy life should be available equally for everyone. Governments must take on the responsibility of ensuring that we live in a socially equal society. Not only is this fair but it also pushes nations forward in their economic and technological progress.

While studying engineering, Rohini became aware of the growing importance of technology in our society. More and more Indians were accessing the Internet and owning digital devices.

Today the topic that Rohini likes to study the most is the intersection between law, government and technology. Rohini is an independent researcher. She doesn't conduct her research as part of any university or research institute. Sometimes, she teams up with non-governmental organizations or NGOs, universities and research bodies, but she is free to pursue the work she wants to do without anyone telling her what to study. She does not have a PhD, but this doesn't stop her from publishing her findings in journals like any other researcher.

'I am a researcher in my own right. People think that a researcher is only someone who peers through lab equipment at big institutions. But there are several independent researchers like me who employ scientific methods to investigate certain questions and the goal is always to make human life better in some way or the other,' she says.

Rohini is one of the very few researchers in the country campaigning to make technology accessible to all Indians. Her goal is to ensure that no one is left behind as the country moves forward. As millions of Indians buy and use devices to log on to the Internet, a large online community is being created. It is through this that more and more Indians choose to stay connected. The Web is used as a library of knowledge that can be accessed from anywhere. However, Rohini's research shows that this access to knowledge is not evenly distributed. And many people still have no access to the Internet even though technology itself does not differentiate between people.

For example, information on the most commonly used websites is in English. In a country like India, where only a small percentage of the population is fluent in English, these apps/websites are of limited use. This limited access to information is made worse in case of complete Internet shutdowns by governments during times of political tension. Rohini has recently researched the impact of one such Internet shutdown on the lives of women in Manipur to show how it affects their lives negatively.

According to Rohini, before making websites, apps, mobile phones and tablets, the ethnographic make up—all the different types of people that might use the product—should be studied. She believes that right from the starting point of making any software, hardware or digital content, creators of the technology should be aware of the different kinds of people that might use it. This is the only way everyone will have equal open and free access to our collective knowledge through the Internet.

Translating existing content is one way to go, but Rohini believes we should go one step further. Rather than using technology that is made in Europe and America, home-grown technology made by Indians, for Indians, will suit us better, don't you think? Rohini sure does.

Further, the few existing apps and websites available in other Indian languages such as Tamil, Hindi, Bengali and Urdu are not easily discoverable. Even the devices you can buy in the market to access the Internet serve only a small section of people. For example, the visually impaired, who read by touch and not with their eyes, have hardly any options. The elderly and the physically disabled cannot use a smartphone that is made for the mythical 'average human being' in mind.

When new inventions are made, they can be officially registered as 'unique' and 'new' with the country's patent offices. For one of her studies, Rohini counted the patents that Indian and foreign mobile phone companies had filed. She was surprised to see that no patents had been filed by the Indian companies with respect to actual hardware or software that is fundamental to the phone, such as its processor or its Internet capabilities. The few patents she found were for value-added services like caller tunes. She found that Indian mobile phone manufacturers were only assembling the parts in India; the manufacture and design of the products took place elsewhere in the world—China and Europe/North America, respectively.

According to Rohini, all the benefits that technology has to offer to us can be truly utilized to its full potential only if we make technology with Indian culture, languages and the diversity of our country in mind, keeping it accessible to all.

VANITA
PRASAD

Environmental biotechnologist

Managing waste coming out from industries, bazaars and houses is a big challenge for India. Vanita, the microbe doctor, has a bright old idea that can help.

INVENTING A MICROBE MIX THAT CLEANS

As a little girl, Vanita suffered from severe headaches. Worried about their daughter's health, her parents brought her to a big hospital in Delhi. At the hospital, twelve-year-old Vanita got her brain scanned. The doctors asked her to lie down on a bed that was pulled into a big machine that could see inside her head. Vanita was amazed to see and feel the machine interacting with her body. The moment she entered the majestic CT scan machine, she fell in love with science. *I want to know how the human body works. I want to invent new technology like this*, the young Vanita thought to herself.

The desire to invent things never left her. Years later, she attempted to invent a test that shows doctors everything that a patient is allergic to. She soon realized that people were allergic to too many diverse things like pollen, peanuts and many chemicals. All of these could not fit into one single test. Then, an even bigger problem caught her attention: hygiene. A visit to a big vegetable market inspired another idea in Vanita's mind. *What happens to all the vegetables, fruits and flowers that no one buys? Where does all the waste go? Can we make the waste useful?* she wondered.

She had studied biotechnology by then. She knew wet waste could be used to produce bio-hydrogen or 'the future fuel', as Vanita calls it.

Today, Vanita works with a natural process to break waste down. It is an old technique but Vanita has upgraded it. In a process called anaerobic digestion, waste is 'digested' by bacteria that do not need oxygen to live. As a result, waste is broken down and energy is released. By mixing the waste with the right bacteria in a closed chamber that has no oxygen, this natural process has been turned into technology to convert waste into useful energy very fast. It is a 'win-win' solution that a large country like India really needs.

This technology has been used in gobar gas plants in India since the 1930s at least. Organic waste from kitchens, toilets and farms in villages have been digested in closed chambers to make local biogas useful for cooking.

Vanita believes this technology can be taken much further and also be used to treat industrial waste. But for large-scale application, this technology must be made much more efficient and easier to use. The efficiency can be boosted if the right bacteria are used and their health is checked regularly. The result will be even better if multiple bacteria that work together perfectly to get the job done are chosen. Vanita's new twist is to make a perfect recipe of microbes. She has prepared a mixture of more than 650 different bacteria. They have names like acidogens, acetogens and methanogens.

India is home to more than a billion people. The amount of waste generated in our vegetable markets, toilets, kitchens and factories increases every year. This is a big problem because untreated waste, if not disposed of properly, can contaminate clean water and spread disease. All this waste, if put to use smartly, as Vanita plans to, can provide local energy that does not pollute. Recognizing this, the Indian government gave Vanita a big grant to take this work further.

Vanita's mixture of bacteria is very special for three reasons. First, this mixture is clumpy and dry—many industrial digesters currently use a liquid mixture of microbes that choke up the digesters. Second, this mixture works well for large-scale treatment of solid waste and waste water from industries. Third, Vanita, has chosen waste-eating bacteria that work well together to make a perfect blend. She knows a lot about all these microbes. She even calls herself 'the microbe doctor'.

She has tested her clumpy dry microbe mixture thoroughly, in her lab in Baroda, Gujarat, to treat waste water from industries. A ten-litre bioreactor—a chamber for 'digestion' to take place—works every day in Vanita's lab. All the pollutants in the waste are eaten up and nothing but reusable water is left behind. It doesn't even need electricity to run! In fact, clean fuel comes out of the reaction as a by-product.

To make her recipe famous, Vanita started a company. She recently bought a piece of land to build a much bigger bioreactor with a volume of twenty-cubic-metres. Now she can produce and sell her recipe of microbes to the people in India who need it. She believes this technology, with all her new add-ons, can be useful on a large-scale in multiple locations in the country including in cities and industrial complexes. Vanita's dream is indeed coming true.

 Glossary

1. **Anaerobic digestion:** The process by which certain microorganisms digest organic material, like plant and animal materials, in the absence of oxygen and produce gases as a byproduct that can be used as fuel.

2. **Biogas:** The gas produced as a result of breakdown of organic matter like plant and animal material.

3. **Chromosome:** Bundles of genetic material packaged together in molecules inside the nucleus of each cell. Humans have 46 chromosomes, spinach has 12!

4. **Climate change:** Changes in the earth's climate that affect the heat, wind, ocean currents and rain patterns. The climate crisis is a huge threat to the biodiversity on the planet. Human activities in the recent industrial age and unchecked commercialization are the causes for this.

5. **CT Scan machine:** The computer tomography scan machine is tunnel-shaped and can scan an object with X rays from different angles to produce slice images without cutting the object.

6. **Eco-friendly menstruation:** Sanitary pads and tampons, the most common products used during menstruation (or 'periods'), are non-biodegradable. They pollute the environment after disposal as they persist for thousands of years! Alternatives like menstrual cups and cloth napkins are more eco-friendly, safe and hygienic, and environmentalists love them.

7. **Enzyme:** A protein produced in cells that is useful in accelerating chemical reactions.

8. **Epicentre:** The point on the earth's surface at which an earthquake originates and where the tremors are the strongest.

9. **Gene:** A gene is a part of the DNA in our chromosomes and codes for a specific function. Not all DNA make up genes but genes are made up of DNA. A gene might be a short piece of DNA or it could be very long.

10. **Grant:** A chunk of funds that might be money or resources provided to carry out a specific research project or task.

11. **Microorganism:** An organism that is so small that it cannot be seen with the naked eye. Example: bacteria

12. **Prime number:** A whole number (greater than 1), which cannot be made by multiplying other whole numbers. Example: 2, 3, 7, 23

13. **Quantitative science:** A scientific study that uses definite statistical, mathematical and computational systems.

14. **Sociology:** The study of the history, development and functioning of human society.
15. **Star system:** All the planets, moons and other cosmic bodies around a star.
16. **Thermodynamics:** The study of heat in relation to energy and other properties of matter.
17. **Tissue:** A tissue is a group of cells that look similar and act together to perform a specific task. Many tissues make up an organ. Example: skin tissue
18. **Ultraviolet light:** A type of radiation or light from the sun that is responsible for tanning our skin. Exposure for too long, over time, can cause cancer.

● ◆ ●

Acknowledgements

This book could not have been made without the encouragement we received from our friends, family and the community of brave and inspiring women in science that we met during our travels. Thank you to the thirty-one fantastic scientists featured in this book, who were so generous with their time, ideas and support for this book. It was certainly a shot in the arm for us that they were as passionate as we were about making complex and contemporary science accessible to a wider and younger audience.

We are grateful to Ria Rajan, whose art first opened our eyes to what this book could be. We would like to extend our gratitude to Kiran Mazumdar-Shaw for supporting us with writing fellowships while we worked on this book. Additionally, we would like to thank our crowdfunding contributors for helping us to continue producing feminist science media content for our website while we worked on this book. Special shout-outs to Mukund Thattai, Yasmin Khan, Amita Chebbi and Dinesh Thakur.

• ✦ •

•

In memoriam ✦

Many Indian women reached great heights in research in times when women in science were a rarity. They opened the doors for those profiled in this book.

Asima Chatterjee (1917–2006)

She was a chemist known for her research on chemicals called alkaloids, as well as for discovering drugs that treat epilepsy and malaria.

Veronica Rodrigues (1953–2010)

Although born in Kenya, she did her breakthrough research in India. She was a pioneer in our understanding of how smell and taste sensory neurons develop.

Anna Mani (1918–2001)

A renowned expert on Indian weather, she dedicated her life to weather measurements and to designing gadgets that could do this efficiently.

C. Parvathamma (1927–2006)

As a sociologist who studied the status of scheduled castes and tribes, her critique of Brahmanical scholarly superiority is valuable in understanding the social realities of our country.

Janaki Ammal (1897–1984)

Janaki Ammal was a botanist who made several hybrids that contributed hugely to the food security and economic challenges of a young India after independence. The national awards on taxonomy are named after her.

Kalpana Chawla (1962–2003)

Kalpana Chawla was an astronaut born in Karnal, Haryana. She went to space twice, to carry out research on astronaut safety and health. Sadly, she passed away on her way back to earth with her six crew members when their space shuttle disintegrated.

Read More in Puffin

The Girl Who Went to the Stars: and Other Extraordinary Lives

Ishita Jain and Naomi Kundu

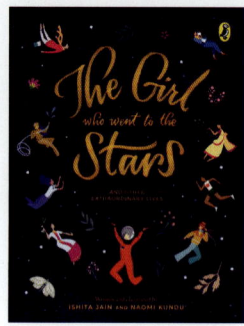 **An unbelievable journey through outer space, the voice of a nightingale, a climb up the highest mountain in the world, a leader of the nation!**

The Girl Who Went to the Stars and Other Extraordinary Lives is a collection of incredible stories that teach passion and courage. These Indian women followed their dreams, however difficult they seemed, and showed us that we can be anything we want to be.

So whether you're a girl or a boy, big or small, short or tall—immerse yourself in the world of India's most loved and admired women, who were once kids just like you!

Read More in Puffin

Become a Junior Inventor

Cloud Mentor

Imagine, Invent, Engineer!

Ever wondered how roller coasters work? Been fascinated with solar panels and windmills, batteries and switches, wires and bulbs? Get acquainted with these movers and shakers of the world of gadgetry around us . . . and become a junior inventor yourself!

Written by Cloud Mentor, a company that mentors kids to become budding inventors, this fun book features almost every conceivable topic of interest—from machines and circuits to structural innovations and design basics. Learn how to make a waterwheel, create your own bottle boat at home and explore the science behind your favourite toy.